Visit us at www.boldstrokesbooks.com

A RETURN TO ARMS

By the Author

Let the Lover Be

A Return to Arms

A RETURN TO ARMS

by

Sheree L. Greer

2016

A RETURN TO ARMS
© 2016 By Sheree L. Greer. All Rights Reserved.

ISBN 13: 978-1-62639-681-4

This Trade Paperback Original Is Published By
Bold Strokes Books, Inc.
P.O. Box 249
Valley Falls, NY 12185

First Edition: March 2016

Credits
Editor: Cindy Cresap
Production Design: Susan Ramundo
Cover Design By Jeanine Henning

Acknowledgments

I spent a lot of time either crying or on the verge of tears as I wrote this book. I spent a lot of time cussing and a lot of time silent. I am extremely thankful for a number of people in my life who gave me their shoulder, their ear, their encouragement, and their perspectives. I name a few here, but know that my community is wide and my love runs deep for all of you.

Thank you Jasmine Smith, Fiona Lewis, Khaulah Nuruddin, Adrien Julious, Tiffany Wilson, Pamela Wilson, Wilbert Wilson, and Orlando Pizana.

Dedication

For my mother, who held me after the Trayvon Martin verdict, who comforted me through my tears, my rage, and my frustration, who told me hopelessness is not an option.

BOOK I

Chapter One

"Take off your clothes," Folami said. She stood naked at the foot of her bed, hands on her shapely hips, afro a big, bold frame for her smoldering brown eyes and glossed lips.

Toya, who had just entered the studio apartment, stood stunned near the front door. Folami had texted her to come over, never mind the lateness of the hour, telling her in a follow-up message that the door would be open. The apartment was small, decorated like a revolutionary's love nest. Malcolm X and Garvey posters hanging on the walls, a red and black area rug covering the terrazzo floor of the main living area, and a Kente cloth draped over the large window near her futon, which Folami always left unmade and in bed position. The dim apartment smelled of incense, a soothing mixture of sandalwood and myrrh.

"Did I stutter?" Folami said. She cocked her head to the side and crinkled her brow in challenge. She flexed her toned arms, rolling her shoulders back and forth, as she spread her legs a little farther apart. Toya stared at her thick thighs before stepping out of her sneakers.

Toya ran a hand over her short, tight curls before stepping more fully into the room, which was only lit with pillar candles on the small table near the bed and a desk lamp with a thin red cloth draped over the shade. Toya's eyes adjusted to the darkness, the dancing shadows and soft orange-yellow haze that bathed the room. She unbuckled her belt, unbuttoned her jeans, and pulled her zipper down. She stopped. Toya took a deep breath and stared at Folami. Still, all these months after their first meeting, Folami's beauty stopped Toya completely, caught her and held her hostage.

"What?" Folami asked, her eyes bright with anticipation. The candlelight flickered across her bare breasts and shoulders, kissing the curves of her face.

"I'm glad you invited me over," Toya said, the words light and playful when they came out of her mouth, the ease of it like cotton candy melting on her tongue. She had been in a heavy, suffocating mood before hearing from Folami. Thinking too much about her past, the voicemail from her mother that she refused to listen to, and thinking too much about current events, the shooting of an unarmed Black teen in Evergreen, Florida.

Folami smiled. "I'm glad you came." She stepped forward and grabbed Toya's belt buckle. She pulled her closer.

"It's good to hear you say that," Toya said. "It's nice."

"Don't start, okay?" Folami said. She slid her hand into Toya's pants. "Don't ruin it."

"Don't ruin it" was one of Folami's refrains when it came to Toya. The moment would be just right, a kiss, a touch, a moment of openness and intimacy. Just when Toya would want to name it, capture it, and cradle it against her chest, Folami would say, "don't ruin it" and confirm that the moment was nothing more than a therapeutic ritual and most certainly not a romantic coming together, the bulkiness between them a large, jagged rock balancing on one of its points.

Toya started to turn away, but Folami grabbed her chin and pulled her into a kiss. Folami's tongue was magic; the way it plunged and flittered, curled and teased, coupled with the movement of her fingers in Toya's pants was like a sleight of hand trick. A trick that made all Toya's doubts and questions disappear, not gone, but temporarily out of sight.

They made love. Slow at first, a tenderness to their touching that reminded Toya of her first time, a summer, winter, and spring break love affair with her neighbor's daughter, a college freshman at FAMU. A young and excited high school junior at the time, Toya followed her lover's lead with a subdued mix of uncertainty about her feelings but determined desire to please. The same passionate energy rose up in her whenever she and Folami got together, and though she was miles away from the Milwaukee neighborhood she grew up in and years ahead of being that sexually-confused and tormented adolescent, she still felt a certain anxiety that made her tremble at Folami's touch.

When Toya finally stopped thinking about what it all meant, what would become of them, where their love was going, even letting go of all that was happening in the world, when Toya was able to shake loose everything, she broke free and dove into Folami with all she had, and Folami opened herself up, made herself more available. A spreading of legs, an invitation for Toya to have her way. The lovemaking picked up pace; an urgency burst between them, a raging heat consuming Toya from the inside. Only Folami had the power to cool her, calm her, and so Toya clung to her with hands and mouth, holding her, drinking her.

Out of breath and wrapped in each other's arms, Toya and Folami lay in silence. Toya knew she'd be the first to break it even as she waited for Folami to speak first. A tire screeched in the distance and a screaming siren followed soon after. Toya sighed. The noise of the sirens chased away Toya's thoughts about her and Folami and what she was going to say.

"Even just hearing the police fills me with dread and rage," Toya said. "Without even thinking about what the circumstances might be, I'm just filled with anger and fear. Every time." She lifted Folami's hand and placed it above her breast, right over her heart.

"I know," Folami said in a whisper. "I feel it too. And with the J'Quan Miles shooting, I just don't know how much more I can take." She turned and hugged Toya close to her.

The latest police shooting was one of the reasons she was so relieved to get Folami's text. Toya had been lying in bed, staring at the ceiling, thinking about death, thinking about J'Quan Miles.

The story could have been kept quiet, like many stories of murder are kept quiet in small towns with one local news station, one strip mall, and no university, but with the help of the Black Lives Matter movement and social media, this one had gone viral. The off-duty deputy Eric Vaughn, who shot J'Quan Miles, claimed self-defense. He said Miles was attempting to break into a neighboring house, that he had been watching him walk toward the end of the block, and since he slowed down in the middle of the block, looking at the dark, closed up house of a family that happened to not be home, he knew Miles was up to something. Vaughn said when he announced himself and interrupted the crime, J'Quan attacked him. He claimed J'Quan reached for a gun. Rumor had it, based on a surveillance video of him leaving a gas station around the corner, that all he had was a bag of green apple Frooties. After it happened, Vaughn went home and called it in. The body was picked up and the scene taped off within the hour. Other than reports of J'Quan's wailing, barefoot mother, clad in a pale yellow bathrobe and satin bonnet, pacing up and down the block where her son had been gunned down, not much was known about the night in question. What they did know, and what incensed them most of all, was that Vaughn had yet to be charged.

"What are we going to do?" Toya asked. "What can we do? Everything we do seems so...so futile." She kissed Folami's forehead.

Folami sat up. She looked down at Toya. "Don't say that."

"Don't say what? The obvious?" Toya returned Folami's stare.

"Don't say it's futile," Folami said. "We're doing good work at RiseUP!, Toya. We're just beginning and we got a lot of work to do, true, but we're on the right track."

"Listen at you. All optimistic and shit." Toya smiled. They did do good work at RiseUP!, the community center where Toya met Folami. They worked alongside two other active members, Fishbone and Kanaan, to create social action committees and community action events. Earlier in the week, the four of them led a nice committee of concerned citizens and activists eager to exchange ideas and organize around the recent shootings plaguing South St. Petersburg. The work, challenging but important, had been leaving Toya feeling a bit ineffective as of late, but Folami's hope and determination, her fortitude even in the face of what seemed insurmountable was one of the things she loved about her. Love. She loved Folami. She wanted to say it. She pushed herself up on her elbows.

Folami tapped her lips with her short, glossy red-painted fingernails. "You do raise an interesting point though." She narrowed her eyes. "We need more people on the ground floor. We need people to feel connected to what's going on."

"Okay," Toya said. "More connected than the meetings at the center?"

"I got it!" Folami bounced and clapped her hands together. "We can make a series of short videos! Each one showcasing the recent shootings." She talked with her hands, tapping Toya's bare shoulder then gripping it as the idea took shape. "And not just the ones here. We'll talk about everybody from Tamir Rice to Tanisha Anderson! Eric Garner to Rekia Boyd!"

Toya nodded. "Sounds like you're on to something."

"On to something? This shit is brilliant!" Folami shook Toya's shoulder in excitement.

"Brilliant?" Toya raised an eyebrow.

"Yes, brilliant." Folami slapped Toya's shoulder.

"Ouch!" Toya frowned.

"Think about it, Toya. So much of this is about information and creating an urgency. We all got numbers on our heads if we think about it. Anyone of us could be next! That's the urgency! That's the horrific truth of it!" Folami jumped from the bed and scrambled to her desk. Her naked thighs and ass jiggling slightly as she moved. She grabbed a stack of note cards and a black Sharpie then hunched over the desk to start writing. "We'd need a name for it, but the concept is simple. We can give biographical information and summarize the cases. Can you print large pictures of the victims? You can do that at work, right? Just big pictures of them for me to hold up on camera. You should print them on poster board! I mean big, close-up shots of their faces. What do you call them? When the pictures are just big and in your face?" She turned to Toya. Her eyes wide and electric, her naked body almost trembling with excitement.

"Portraits?" Toya said. She shrugged and raised an eyebrow.

"Yeah," Folami said. "Portaits! Large portraits!" She turned back to her note cards to keep writing.

Toya lay back. She listened to Folami mumble to herself as she scribbled notes. She could still say it. She could get up and walk up behind Folami, take her in her arms, and whisper "I love you" against her shoulder. She glanced over at Folami, who had spread her tank top on the seat of the wooden desk chair and sat down. She was in her own world now, a place where nothing mattered but the work. A place Toya already knew her profession of love would be unwelcome. She sat up and pushed herself from the futon.

"It's a good idea," Toya said, joining Folami at the desk. "A really good idea."

Chapter Two

Toya leaned against the counter at Copy Pros, the small printing company that hired her part-time. She hoped for full-time at some point, the last bit of money she had from selling her car would soon be gone, and she'd finally feel the real pinch of her parents cutting her off. Toya tried to stay hopeful about it. The job was easy, the people were nice, and she was able to work with RiseUP! and do her photography without a hassle. Toya split her shift with the owner's son Thelonius, an interracial teenager who seemed to take after his Black mother, who he mentioned rarely but with reverence. He said, proudly, that his name, curly hair, and dark eyes were from her, as was his love of all things related to Blues and Jazz. His father, Mr. Aaron, was a kind, thoughtful man who inherited the print shop from his father. The place had limited hours, closed on Sundays and Mondays, and Toya mentioned to Mr. Aaron often that she wouldn't mind working full-time.

A printer in the back beeped loudly, the alert for low paper, and she went to tend to it. Just as she turned, the bells above the entrance jingled.

"Hey," Folami said. She walked in smiling, a long green maxi dress hugging her hips.

"Hey, yourself," Toya said. She dashed back to the beeping printer, opened the bottom drawer with a rattling yank, and filled the printer with card stock from an open box near her feet. Having reset the drawer, she tapped the resume button. The printer clunked then returned to the rhythmic swoosh, click, swoosh that would soon fade into the background.

"Slow in here today, I see." Folami looked around. The two self-service computers sat empty, and the long table for sorting held only an empty box, a pen, and a single manila folder.

Toya sighed. "It's slow most days," she said. "It picks up on Saturday, and some when school's in session. But during these mid-summer weeks? Nothing." She leaned her elbows on the counter and rested her chin on her fists. "Only customer I had today was a woman printing signs for her rummage sale."

"Rummage sale?" Folami laughed. "You mean a yard sale?"

Toya shook her head and chuckled. Folami always teased her for her Midwestern terminology. She had been in Florida a little over two years, but still held tight to her language, soda was still pop and a water fountain was still a bubbler. "Whatever," she said.

"Well, I came by to see if you could show me some size options for the portraits. I'm thinking big, but not so big that they would be awkward for me to hold up on the video."

"Yeah, I can show you some sizes." Toya stood up and put her hands on her hips. "I'm surprised you want to use portraits though. The way you think video trumps photography and all that." She raised her eyebrow and smirked. It's something they debated often—photographs versus video, which made the bigger statement, created the most impact. Stills took the moment and froze it for contemplation. You could look at a photograph, a single moment, a single action or gesture, and the world stopped for a second, demanded that you think. Folami, on the other hand, thought the silence of a photograph was too inactive. She said that the sound and movement of video made the moment, whatever was happening, come alive, made you have to face it as it happened. "Pictures are nice," Folami always said, "but film is life."

Folami rolled her eyes and smiled. "First, I still believe film trumps photography. But I didn't say photos were useless, and for this, the images are going to be a great complement to what we'll be filming." She shrugged and folded her arms in satisfaction.

"Complement, huh?" Toya turned from the counter and made her way to the large metal shelf of sample poster boards, tri-fold displays, and foam boards. She grabbed a couple different sized poster and foam boards to show Folami.

"The main narrative is the film," Folami said. "The message is going to be in the information."

"The narrative is their faces. Being able to look into Kathryn Johnston's eyes, John Crawford's eyes, Aiyana Jones's eyes. And then those eyes staring right back at you." Toya spread the assorted boards on the counter. "The information is the caption, Folami. The message is the faces."

"Whatever," she said. "We'll see about that tonight when we do a test run. Without the portraits. It's gonna be heavy. Trust." She eyed the foam boards. She picked one up and held it in front of her. She closed one eye and tilted her head. "This size is perfect!"

Toya took the twenty-by-thirty-inch foam poster board from her. "At this size, you're going to totally prove my point. The portraits are going to steal the show," she said, visualizing the perfect way to print the images. Black-and-white. Dramatic. Some of the images she'd already shot from various RiseUP! meetings, and most of the shots she'd gotten from four funerals over the past six weeks, were all RAW files, more dynamic, sharper than .jpegs. She'd be able to blow them up nicely, really capture the texture and lines of the faces, an honesty of expression in the skin imperfections and starkness of the eyes.

"I see that look," Folami said. "You're up to something."

"No, I'm not." Toya put the foam board aside and stacked up the rejects on the counter to return to the shelf. "I just know this is going to be beautiful."

"It is. Beautiful and important." Folami nodded and stepped closer to the counter.

"Like we are. Beautiful and important." Toya leaned on the counter.

Folami sighed and took a step back.

"I mean 'we' in the larger context," Toya said. "Us as in our community. The collective 'we,' so you can save your eye roll."

"I didn't roll my eyes."

"But you wanted to," Toya said. "I can tell."

"You don't know me." Folami smiled and walked toward the counter again. She pressed herself against it. She looked around the empty store. Toya followed her gaze. Large, lonely photocopiers and empty desktops. Plastic blue bins filled with abandoned jobs and mistakes. Folami returned her stare to Toya, who looked into her eyes and ignored the flutter in her belly.

"I think I do," Toya said. "Or at least I'm getting pretty close." She took a deep breath and leaned forward slightly, wanting to fill the space between them but not wanting to give in completely.

Folami stretched herself across the counter. She held on to the rounded edge of it and pushed her weight forward. Curious to see if Folami would go through with it, Toya didn't move. Folami didn't do public displays of affection, all the passion and romance between them regulated to the private intimacy of her apartment. Folami stretched forward more and kissed Toya on the mouth, a hard, full press of soft, strawberry scented lips. She jumped back, landing on her sandaled feet with a hop.

"Did you know I was going to do that?" She smiled.

Toya cleared her throat. Stunned. "No. No, I didn't."

"Good," Folami said. "See you at the center later. We'll do a test run and maybe check out some of the images you already have?"

"Sounds good," Toya said.

"We make a good team, Toya," Folami said. "And when I say 'we' I mean 'we.' You and me." She winked and turned. She waved her hand in the most nonchalant of gestures and pushed through the door.

Toya watched her walk past the windows and around the corner to the parking lot. She shook her head then licked her lips. Strawberries.

CHAPTER THREE

Toya and Folami sat on the porch at the RiseUP!
Community Center. The center, a converted house in
desperate need of a paint job, had been a part of the Harbordale
community for decades. First, a small gathering place for Director
Abasi and other ex-Panthers, it used to be a halfway house for
young men transitioning from jail back into the community, then
became a place of community action.

They sat shoulder to shoulder, hip to hip, with Folami leaning
over to look at the screen on Toya's camera.

"When did you take these?" Folami asked.

"At the Johnston memorial service," Toya said. She advanced
the photos. Shots of a family in mourning. In some of the photos,
men and women held each other's hands and stared down at the
ground, heads bowed in prayer and grief. In others, men and
women, dressed in black, held signs: "Stop State Sanctioned
Murder" and "Shame on YOU" with pictures of officers from the
Atlanta Police Department website. One particularly compelling
shot made Folami gasp. A young girl, no more than nine with
tears welled in both eyes and her bottom lip held between her
teeth, sat in the grass near the casket. The girl's eyes looked
straight ahead, directly into the camera.

"I can't...I can't even begin to..." Folami wiped her eyes
then looked away.

"I know," Toya said. She put the camera down at her feet and pulled Folami close to her. "It was a hard day." Toya took a deep breath, remembering the story and fighting back her own tears. During a botched drug raid, a Black woman, Kathryn Johnston, was killed by plainclothes officers who broke down her door in a no-knock raid. She fired her gun at the intruders, and the police filled her with bullets. The funeral was both a home-going and a rally, sorrowful farewell, and defiant protest. When an investigation revealed that the police falsified affidavits and planted drug evidence in the elderly woman's home to cover up the murder, the city responded with calls for justice.

"Thirty-nine shots. Thirty-nine." Folami's voice caught in her throat. "You know those officers are back on the street," she whispered.

Toya sighed. "It's like you said, we gotta get the word out. We have to let people know what's going on." She squeezed Folami's shoulder and picked her camera back up. "Come on. Showtime. Let's do a test run."

Folami wiped her face again and stood up. She stretched her back and shoulders, rolling her head and breathing deeply. "Okay," she said. "Okay."

Toya pushed herself from the wooden steps. She bent down to get the tripod out of her bag and set it up, sliding the legs out and snapping the bridge in place. As she picked up the camera to attach it to the top of the stand, a Toyota Camry, gleaming and glowing in sour apple green, screeched to a stop. The car trembled with bass and sunlight bounced off the gold rims. The back passenger door opened, a chopped and screwed version of Erykah Badu's "On and On" poured onto the curb and seemed to ooze all over the sidewalk and crabgrass. Fishbone stretched himself out of the car. He raised a fist while walking up to Toya and Folami.

"Peace, Queens," Fishbone said, his voice a perpetual whisper. Tall, bony, with an unruly head of dreads, the sizes and lengths varying without method or management, Fishbone spent most of his time with RiseUP! writing poems and performing at open mics. His voice, gritty and unassuming, and the way he swayed his body while he recited his verses hypnotized audiences from St. Petersburg to Atlanta.

"What it do?" He smiled and pulled up his baggy jeans. They slipped right back down to where they had been, belted but low on his narrow hips.

"Hey, Fish." Folami turned to look back at the car at the curb. The bass still trembled; the engine idled.

"What's up?" Toya said. She returned her attention to setting up the camera.

"I can't call it," Fishbone said. "I brought this flyer design so you can make the copies." He dug in the pocket of his oversized jeans and produced a small thumb drive. He tossed it to Toya.

Toya caught it. "Cool," she said. "I'll print them tomorrow." She slid the drive into her hip pocket.

"Yup," Fishbone said. "What y'all doing?"

"We about to make a video," Folami said.

"More like a screen test," Toya said over her shoulder.

"I'm not auditioning," Folami said.

Toya threw a quick glance at Fishbone then raised her eyebrow at Folami. "Says who?"

"Whatever!" She kicked Toya in the butt playfully. "We're doing a series of videos where we give summaries of all the police fuckery. The brutality and cover-ups. The murders. Just all the bullshit."

"Get all the cussing out. We need clean, family-friendly language. I want people from eight to eighty to watch these things." Toya adjusted the camera on the tripod and stood behind the viewfinder.

"That's real cool, y'all. Respect." Fishbone nodded.

"People have to know that these aren't isolated incidents. The shit—" Folami stopped.

Toya raised her head and twisted her lips.

"The cases are all related," Folami said. "All evidence of the systematic and oppressive police state we living in. That's what it is, you know. We in a damn police state."

Toya and Fishbone nodded in agreement.

"But what we gonna do about it though?" Fishbone said. He looked over his shoulder at the green car.

Folami and Toya followed his eyes. Kanaan, a fellow activist who spent much of his time working with RiseUP! outreach and membership drives, pushed open the passenger side door of the car but didn't get out. Badu's voice, slow and sweet as honey, drizzled all over the bass and snare of the music that crept out of the open passenger door. Kanaan talked excitedly to the driver, shaking his head and moving his hands. Folami, Toya, and Fishbone looked at each other and shrugged.

Kanaan finally stepped out of the car, his bright, multi-colored dashiki glowing against the faded gray of his oversized jeans. He gave Folami, Toya, and Fishbone a head nod before turning back to the car. He held the passenger door open and told the driver, a woman in large sunglasses, to stay in the car. He slammed the door and walked up the cement path to where Toya, Folami, and Fishbone stood.

"Hotep, Queens," Kanaan said to Folami with a smile. He folded his arms across his chest, dreads pulled back into a ponytail, and a licorice root chewstick in the corner of his mouth. He wore silver, mirrored aviators, even though Toya had told him on several occasions they were the sunglasses of choice for Florida state troopers.

He gave Folami a one-armed hug. "Good to see you, sis," he said. "You, too, LaToya," he added.

Toya cut her eyes at him. She didn't like Kanaan, and the fact that he accidentally-on-purpose called her by her full name every chance he got didn't help. Hearing "LaToya" always made Toya think of her parents. They never shortened her name and had even disapproved of the abbreviated version. "If we wanted your name to be Toya, we would have named you Toya," her father always said. Her mother, who always seemed to quietly cosign her husband's sentiments, had nodded, her lips flat against her teeth, her eyebrows furrowed in seriousness. Toya shook away thoughts of her parents and glared at Kanaan.

"I mean, Toya," Kanaan said. He chuckled. "You real sensitive, you know that?" He stood next to Fishbone, who snickered and yanked up his pants.

"Kanaan," Toya said. She forced a tight-lipped smile and moved back to the viewfinder, adjusting the zoom and applying settings for shooting video.

"What y'all got going?" Kanaan asked.

Folami filled Kanaan in, and Toya continued working with the settings on the camera. Kanaan nodded his approval while glancing back over his shoulder at the green Camry as if to make sure the woman hadn't left. The bass thumped. The car hadn't moved.

"So, the videos will have talking points, too," Folami said. "Things for people to consider going forward, you know?"

"I got you, Queen," Kanaan said. "It's a cute idea."

"Cute?" Folami said. She put a hand on her hip.

"Yeah, cute." He shrugged. He elbowed Fishbone, who whistled through his blunt-brown lips. "Look," Kanaan said, "the videos might get a few hits, but do you really think they gon' reach the masses? You think they gon' mobilize the soldiers? The people doing the real work ain't on YouTube." He chuckled.

"You're wrong," Toya said. She tilted the camera forward with both hands and checked something on the monitor before tapping buttons with her thumb.

"What?" Kanaan said. He slid his sunglasses off his face and screwed his face, his full lips twisting in challenge. "You think people sitting at they computers watching videos with what's going on in these streets?"

"Yeah," Toya said. "They are. Media, social and otherwise, is at the core of this new movement. That 'Last Words' video, you know the one with the last words of unarmed people killed by the police? That got over a million views. Over a million." She tilted the camera back up, leveling it to shoot Folami when she was ready.

Kanaan shook his head and put his sunglasses back on. He chewed on his licorice root then moved it to the other side of his mouth. "Over a million, huh?"

"Kanaan," Fishbone said. "You gotta give it up. That shit was powerful. Them last words were deep. What's that Diallo one?"

"Mom, I'm going to college," Toya and Folami said in unison. They looked at each other and shared a sad smile.

"That shit was brutal," Fishbone said, shaking his dreads and pulling up his pants. "You see that shit, Kanaan?"

"I don't know. Sounds familiar," Kanaan said.

Toya eyed him from behind the camera. Kanaan shrugged and folded his muscular arms across his broad chest. He wore leather bracelets, braided around alternating tiger's-eye stones and cowries. He probably hadn't seen it. He'd never admit that though. According to him, he'd heard of everything, and if he hadn't heard of it, it must not have been important or revolutionary.

"That ain't the point though," he said. "A million views ain't a million people on the front line."

"True," Toya said. "But it contributes to the front line. There's people who saw them words, just those words, and got their minds changed about what this thing means."

Folami and Fishbone nodded. Kanaan chewed his stick then pushed his glasses up. They rested on his forehead. He fixed his brown eyes directly on Toya.

"What we, as Afrikans, have to understand is—"

"KANAAN!" the woman driving the car yelled from the Camry, the passenger window rolled down to reveal the white leather interior of the car. The woman, her hair pulled back into a curly ponytail and bug-eye sunglasses covering most of her face, used the steering wheel for leverage as she leaned across the center console.

"KANAAN! KANAAN!" she called. Erykah Badu's voice, deeper and slower than ever, floated out into the summer heat. It contrasted the woman's loud, flat calls. "KANAAN!"

Kanaan sighed and looked over his shoulder at the woman. He didn't say anything, just turned his back to her. He looked at Folami then Toya. "What we gotta understand is—"

"KANAAN!" the woman yelled again.

Kanaan yanked the stick out of his mouth and whipped around to face the car. "I SAID WAIT A MINUTE! Damn."

Toya and Folami shared the same expression—raised eyebrows and wide eyes. Fishbone fiddled with one of his longest dreads and bit at dry skin on his bottom lip.

"What was I saying?" Kanaan said, slipping the stick into the corner of his mouth and turning back to Toya and Folami.

"What we gotta understand..." Fishbone said under his breath, focused on picking lint from the tip of his dread.

"Why she gotta sit in the car?" Toya asked. She nudged her chin toward the Camry. The window was still halfway down, and the song, apparently on repeat, began again. Keyboard sound effects accompanied the already altered mix of Badu's classic.

Kanaan scrunched his face and dismissed Toya's question with a hand wave. "What we gotta understand is—"

"Good question," Folami said. "We can't meet your friend? Why you making her sit in the car?" She looked over at the green Camry. She lifted her hand to wave. Kanaan lightly slapped it down.

Toya instinctively jumped forward, but Folami smacked Kanaan back on her own. "Don't hit me," Folami said.

Kanaan smiled. "I'm just fucking with you," he said. He glanced over his shoulder. "She gotta sit in the car because I told her to sit in the car."

"But why?" Toya asked.

"Don't worry about her," Kanaan said. "Why you worried about her? Why you so concerned?" He crossed his arms and stared at Toya. He chewed at his stick. "What is it to you she sitting in the car? What that got to do with what we talking about?"

"Man," Fishbone said. "Y'all wild." He pulled his pants up and glanced over at the car. His calm, easygoing demeanor a stark contrast to Kanaan's intensity. He sighed. The woman in the car honked the horn then rolled the window up.

Kanaan clenched his jaw then turned to Fishbone. "Was that the horn? She blowing the fucking horn?" He looked incredulous. He turned to the car and tilted his head to the side.

Toya could imagine what Kanaan's face looked like, and she didn't like it. Kanaan had just moved back to St. Petersburg after spending time in Tallahassee and New York. The first time Toya met him, she didn't care for his attitude. His passion for the work was undeniable, and his knowledge of history impressive, but every word he spoke came out like an admonishment. Every idea or comment biting and divisive, an undercurrent of misogyny, violence, and judgment running beneath every point he made.

"Hey," Fishbone said, "I'm hungry anyway." He rubbed his stomach, his white T-shirt lifting as he made wide exaggerated circles. "Let's go eat."

Kanaan didn't turn around. He continued staring at the car.

"Come on." Fishbone elbowed him in the side.

Kanaan finally turned to Toya and Folami. "Bottom line is views ain't feet." He pulled his sunglasses from his forehead and adjusted them on his nose.

"But they are, and they can be," Toya said, looking at herself in Kanaan's mirrored shades.

"Your idealism is going to get you hurt," Kanaan said.

"What?" Toya said. "You threatening—" She stepped forward, and Folami stopped her with a hand on her chest.

"I mean your feelings," Kanaan said. "Your idealism is going to get your feelings hurt," he said.

"That ain't what you said," Toya said. She gently moved Folami's hand. Her fingers lingered before releasing Folami's wrist.

Kanaan watched the movement and raised an eyebrow at Folami. "But that's what I meant," he said, staring at Toya with a smirk. He looked at Folami. "See how sensitive she is?"

"Come on, man, for real," Fishbone said. "Let's go eat. Damn."

"All right," Kanaan said. "You as impatient as that female in the car!" he said with a chuckle.

"Later, y'all." Fishbone held up his fist and turned to walk toward the car. "Good luck with the video," he said over his shoulder.

"Queens, we out," Kanaan said, nodding at both Toya and Folami. "We'll finish this conversation at another time. There's some key components missing from your position on this media shit." He walked off, and when he got to the car, he yanked the passenger door open. "So we honking horns now?" he said as he climbed in. He slammed the door closed. The car pulled off, the trembling bass and ticking snares trailing off in the distance.

"I don't know why you let him get to you," Folami said. She touched Toya's arm. "Let's do a couple of these videos."

Toya took a deep breath, staring up the street though the car was long gone. "You know he hates women, right?" Toya said.

"He does not," Folami said.

"He does." Toya stood behind the camera and pressed a button before settling down to peer through the viewfinder.

"He doesn't." Folami scrunched her face. "Not all the baby mamas he got. He loves women."

"That's what you make of that?" Toya said. She shook her head. "I don't know, Folami. You brought me into this movement, but I might have to school you on a few things."

"You wish," Folami said. "Just say 'action' or 'go' or whatever." She smiled. "Forget him."

Toya held her hand up for a countdown and chuckled, but the laughter was forced and uneasy.

Chapter Four

Toya picked her pants up from the floor and slid them on. She looked around for her shirt and spotted it hanging off the corner of Folami's desk near the flyers she had come by to drop off, but before she could grab it, Folami sat up in bed and called her out.

"What do you think you're doing?" Folami pulled at the matted sides and back of her afro.

"You were sleep," Toya said.

"But now I'm not," Folami said. "You're leaving? Why?"

Toya turned and zipped up her pants. "I'm just kinda tired. I want to get home before it gets too late. Bus stops running soon." The St. Petersburg buses, although always cool and most times clean, ran slow and sporadically during the week; most routes, even the ones ridden most by work commuters, stopped running in the early evening. Toya remembered the buses in Milwaukee, routes that could get you anywhere in the city. Her parents hated when she took the bus. She did it to spite them, but she mostly enjoyed the people-watching. She would sit in the back and watch people get on and off. She'd take pictures with her mind, imagining the photo essays she could do just based on the tired and triumphant, agitated and affable mix of riders who rode public transportation.

"I don't want you to leave," Folami said. "Stay."

"I was only supposed to be dropping the flyers off anyway!" Toya couldn't help but smile. It was nice for Folami to want her, to say that she wanted her.

"Come on," Folami said. "Stay."

"Why?" Toya put her hands on her hips.

Folami's eyes, full of suggestion and with no trace of apology, roamed Toya's body. Toya folded her arms across her bare breasts. Folami pouted.

"Why?" Toya repeated.

Folami sighed. "I don't know," she said. "I just want you to stay."

Toya shook her head and moved to grab her shirt. She snatched the sleeveless T-shirt, yellow with Bob Marley's face printed across the front in black and brown, and slipped it over her head.

"That's not good enough," Toya said.

"What's wrong?"

"I told you. I'm tired." Toya pulled her shirt down after adjusting it on her shoulders.

"You're upset. Bothered." Folami collapsed on the bed. "I can tell."

Toya took a seat on the edge of the futon mattress.

Toya closed her eyes then looked up at the drop ceiling. She wanted to tell Folami about her mother's message, how she had yet to listen to it. How nervous she was to hear her mother's voice, to really listen to what she had to say after all the time that had passed. Toya's parents had cut her off when she came out to them a couple of years ago, and having made it the past couple of years without them or their money, she wasn't sure they served any purpose for her or her life, or if she even cared about them at all.

Toya sighed. She'd keep it simple. "I've got something to say, but when I say it, I don't want you to make it about something—about someone—that it's not."

Folami sat up. She clutched the sheet, which was probably still damp from their lovemaking, to her chest. "Kanaan. You're still tripping about Kanaan." She rolled her eyes. "I knew it."

"It ain't about him," Toya said. "Not exactly." She exhaled loudly. "It's not about Kanaan. It's not him, but his…type. And it's not just him, because I've seen or experienced that kind of dismissive and discouraging attitude before. The RiseUP! meetings always have a sort of wall to them that I can't penetrate. A sentence gets clipped or a conversation tabled because of who I am. Because of how I am. I see it in their eyes. In their comments when they don't think I'm listening."

"You're being paranoid," Folami said.

"I'm not. It's coded language. All that talk last time about the 'traditional family' and the 'agendas' threatening to weaken our 'families' and 'relationships.' You think I don't know what that shit means? And it's not just about me being a lesbian. It's about being a woman, too! I don't want to have to work with people who—did you hear how Kanaan treated his friend today? A friend who was obviously driving him around all day?"

Folami nodded. "Yeah, but that ain't got nothing to do with us."

"But it does, Folami." Toya stood up. "He treated her like she wasn't shit. Half the time, he speaks to us like we're children, talking down to us like—"

"So it is about Kanaan." Folami sighed and put her head in her hands.

"No," Toya said, balling her hands in frustration. "He's not an anomaly. Attitudes like his run rampant all through RiseUP! It seemed easier to deal with early on, but as we're mobilizing and trying new things to get people engaged, it feels…I don't like it. I don't like the way I feel."

Folami mumbled under her breath.

"What?" Toya said.

"I said, maybe Kanaan is right. You are too sensitive," Folami said without lifting her forehead from the heels of her palm.

Stunned, Toya stared at Folami, her afro still uneven and smashed in places. Folami looked up and met Toya's eyes.

"That's how it is?" Toya said.

She couldn't believe Folami. She had to feel what she felt; it couldn't just be her. As the work gained momentum, Toya felt more and more out of place. In the last meeting before Director Abasi left for Chicago, she and another woman had been talking about doing a Women's Month celebration. The other woman, a third grade teacher at a charter school, presented the idea only to be met with silence. Toya and Folami had chimed in, trying to get everyone else excited about a program honoring the contributions of women in the struggle and even offering workshops on health, finance, and education. Director Abasi had smiled and nodded, only to move on to the next order of business. As she was leaving, the woman approached Toya and Folami on the porch to tell them that Abasi recommended the three of them form a committee to discuss women's issues.

"It's just that there ain't no space in all this for all these 'feelings' and attitudes." Folami slid out of bed and stood beside it, her nakedness an unfair distraction, her loveliness a sucker punch. "It's about the work. It's like Director Abasi said in that first talk. You remember. You remember that first talk, Toya?" She took a step closer to Toya.

"Yeah, I remember. And I don't know that I buy all that shit about dialectical materialism and all that theoretical…game. It's like he's spittin' game," Toya said. "And we sitting there soaking the shit up. I bet half the people in the room that day had no idea what the director was even talking about. And that's what I can't take. Empty rhetoric. It has no…no intersections or complexity. Everything ain't this or that. Nothing is that simple."

"But it is," Folami said. "It is simple. It's the struggle or nothing at all."

"Then the struggle has to include everyone."

"Now you're the one simplifying." Folami reached out and put her hands on Toya's shoulders.

"The shit reminds me of my parents," Toya said. She hadn't meant to, but it just came out.

"Your parents?" Folami scrunched her face in confusion. "What are you talking about? You lost me."

"I told you about my family. My wealthy family back home in Milwaukee." Toya looked at the Garvey poster.

"Yeah, they cut you off when you came out." Folami frowned. "Fucked up. Really fucked up."

"The core of that whole situation is that I didn't fall in line. I didn't fit into the image or whatever that they wanted for me. It was my father really. His word was law in our house. He was judge and jury. My mother? I don't know where she fit. She was always so silent. Always quietly agreeing with everything my father said and did. Even kicking me out and cutting me off. She didn't say a word." Toya exhaled and steeled herself against the anger and sadness that shook her bones. She wiped a tear from her eye.

"I'm sorry, Toya," Folami said. She scooted closer and touched Toya's arm.

"It's nothing," Toya said. She cleared her throat.

"It don't sound like nothing."

"My mother called me." Toya shook her head and looked up at the ceiling.

"What did she say?" Folami said. She leaned in close and gripped Toya's arm.

"I don't know. I didn't listen to the message."

"You gotta listen to it. What if something's wrong?" Folami's eyes widened with concern. She pushed back the side of her afro, tucking a thick curl of hair behind her ear.

"I don't know that I care." Toya eased off the bed.

"You have to listen to the message."

Toya shook her head again. She sighed. "I don't want to."
She shrugged.

"Fine. Don't." Folami snatched the sheets up and situated
them around her.

"Oh, so now you're mad?" Toya said.

"I'm not mad. I'm just irritated. You're being shitty about
Kanaan, you're being shitty about your parents, and somehow
that's equating to the whole movement being shitty? To the work
we're doing with RiseUP! being shitty? Maybe you're just shitty
and your sensitive ass is letting it color everything else. Get over
yourself, Toya." Folami flopped down on the bed.

"What?" Toya said.

"You heard me," Folami said. She sat up then climbed out of
the bed. "Get over yourself."

"I don't need this shit." Toya said, staring Folami down.
She was naked, mad, and gorgeous. Toya blew out a loud breath.
"I don't even know what I'm doing anymore. And this is even
more confusing." She gathered up Folami's body with her eyes,
pulling her close and close and closer still but not really moving.
All intention, no action. "I don't know if I can keep doing this.
Any of it."

"Wait. What are you saying?" Folami asked. "You done with
RiseUP!? Done with me?" She looked pained, but Toya didn't
know what would upset Folami more, quitting the center or
quitting their pseudo-relationship.

"I'm saying..." Toya started then stopped. "I'm saying I'm
tired, and I want to go home."

Folami sat down on the edge of the futon. "Fine. Go."

Toya turned and left, closing the door softly.

BOOK II

CHAPTER FIVE

Folami and Toya sat quietly, alone but together at their favorite restaurant. Hot and nearly empty, the small Jamaican restaurant was sandwiched between a discount meat store and a beauty supply outlet whose only signage consisted of tall, block red letters spelling out WIGS. The restaurant, an inconspicuous south St. Pete favorite, boasted the spiciest, flakiest beef patties in town. Toya's plate a testament to their deliciousness, it overflowed with patties, rice and peas, and two golden plantains. Folami, back on her challenge to "resist eating animal flesh," forked callaloo and dumpling with one hand and scrolled through her phone with the other.

"You want to talk first?" Toya said. They hadn't spoken in a week, a new record since it surpassed the three days they went without speaking when Toya went to visit her parents for the last time.

"Technically, you just did," Folami said, a tentative curl to her lips.

Toya nodded. She picked up a patty and bit into it. Golden flakes of pastry caught on her lip. She licked them off. She had missed Folami and decided on the bus ride to the restaurant that she wouldn't pretend like she hadn't.

"True," she said while chewing. "That makes it your turn."

Folami swallowed the food in her mouth and put her phone down. She took a drink from the ginger beer beside her plate and cleared her throat.

"I asked you to lunch to see if you wanted to move forward with the videos," Folami said. "I reviewed the test spots. They look good but need editing. This project needs you."

"The project needs me," Toya repeated in between bites of her food. She challenged Folami with her eyes. She knew what Folami meant, but was determined to hear her say it. And if Folami couldn't say it, didn't say it, maybe Toya was wrong about it all. Wrong about what was going on between them, wrong about staying with RiseUP!, which she would do if it meant having a strong, supportive relationship with Folami. If it meant them working and fighting together. She couldn't handle the attitudes, the subtle coldness of the others if she had to face it alone.

Folami stared down at her plate. "I'm sorry," she said. She raised her eyes, slowly. "I'm sorry about the other night. I'm tired too. I'm confused too. I know what you meant about some of the attitudes at the center. I've known about them since I started there. It's part of why…" She blinked and licked her lips. "It's part of why I keep my romantic life private. Why I kept us private. There are things to do, and I can't be distracted. The coldness, the suspicion, the ignorance is there, but I work through it."

Toya sighed. "Do you?"

"Yes," Folami said. She frowned with seriousness and concern. "I do. I have to. And I need more women there to help me work against it. We can win against all this shit, Toya. But we have to do it together." She reached her hand across the table. "You know what I mean. You carry shit with you, too."

Toya knew she meant the situation with her parents. She didn't want to think about that. She wanted to focus on her and Folami's relationship, if there was something worth preserving, if they could focus on the work. Maybe she was being too emotional. Perhaps focusing on the work is exactly what she needed all the way around.

"We do have to fight through it." Toya stared down at Folami's outstretched hand and thought about the implicit power and courage of a woman's touch. The softness of Folami's palm, the firm strength of her fingers and flash of her short, neat, crimson-painted nails. Her hand a symbol of exactly what the movement needed—softness and strength. A splash of color. Folami was right. They could win against everything, and there was no victory in quitting. Toya looked into Folami's eyes and back down at her hand and back again. She put her hand on top of Folami's and nodded with a smile.

"Let's do this," Toya said.

"You sure?" Folami asked, squeezing Toya's fingers.

"Yeah," Toya said. She squeezed Folami's hand in return, sealing the agreement. It was time to get serious, to be focused. She knew there was a lot of work to do, and she didn't want to confuse and distract herself worrying about things, and about people, she couldn't change. Folami moved to slide her hand from Toya's grip, but Toya caught it.

"We're doing this together," Toya whispered, surprising herself. "I'm going to work with you, but that's got to be it." She held her breath.

A split second of disappointment flashed across Folami's face, but she quickly chased it away with an affirming but flat smile.

"Something wrong?" Toya wanted Folami to object. Hope expanded in her chest, hot and fragile like blown glass. She thought back to her parents, how she had burst out of the closet to face their disappointment. She couldn't afford to go back there. It would cost her too much. It would cost her everything. And though she loved Folami, she couldn't let her take her back to that place of hiding and shame, dishonesty and frustration.

"No, that's a good idea," Folami said. Her voice caught. She swallowed. "It'll make things easier to navigate if we keep it about the work." She exhaled loudly then pulled her hand away from Toya. She picked up her phone and took a deep breath before swiping the screen and sitting back against the stiff booth.

Toya watched her, knowing Folami wouldn't look at her, and feeling relieved for that. Her eyes, commanding and clear and compelling, would shatter Toya's resolve. She picked up her patty and brought it to her mouth. It was settled then. They would only work together. No more extras. No more late night creeps and early morning secrets. It was settled. She took a bite of her food. She chewed the pastry and ground meat, but all the flavor had gone. She forced the bite down and dropped the remainder of the patty to her plate.

Chapter Six

At first, no one knew what to say. Emotions, at odds since the update, held tongues and hearts captive. Evergreen officials had decided to convene a grand jury rather than arrest Vaughn and charge him based on the police report. The development would make it that much harder to see Vaughn charged in the death of J'Quan Miles. Nothing that came to Toya's mind felt appropriate, nothing seemed productive or particularly useful.

"We need to go there," Folami said. The words landed solid as bricks against the silence in the room.

"Exactly, sis," Fishbone said, nodding. A red bandana held his dreads away from his face. He looked younger and more fragile, his slender face center stage, the bump on the bridge of his nose and long curly lashes pronounced with his hair out of the way.

"I'm ready. I'm ready right now," Folami said. She clapped her hands with finality. The quiet dining room and living room of the RiseUP! center echoed with her excited voice and sharp smack of her palms. Kanaan sat on a folding chair in the living room. He stared at the television like it was a foreign object, his face scrunched in confusion and mouth on the verge of words he wouldn't say.

"Come on! Load up and let's ride out!" Folami shot up from her seat and pushed her chair underneath the table.

"Right now?" Toya asked. She stood near the doorway to the kitchen, half in shadows. Even though she told herself she was ready to get back into the swing of things with RiseUP!, she still held on to the edges, trying to figure out where she fit best. She watched Folami for cues, but her insistence on leaving for Evergreen right that evening struck Toya as premature and reckless.

Folami gathered her shoulder bag, rummaging around, and nodded as she confirmed her phone, wallet, a small notebook, and a small collection of pens.

"Yes. Right now," she said with a shrug. "What's the problem?" She gestured toward the television. The press conference ran once again, this time with commentary from a talking head on cable news. Kanaan reached across to the sofa and grabbed the remote. He muted the voices but remained transfixed on the images flashing across the screen. The victim's father, Juma Miles, at the podium. J'Quan Miles in his hoodie. J'Quan Miles in social media profile pictures, a middle finger to everyone out there who dared judge him, a smile and boyish twinkle in his eye as he posed with his father on a sunny day. The images of J'Quan, varied and random like most pictures of teenagers—J'Quan reveling in that secret rebellion in the privacy of his room, the personas and fantasies, the role playing and posturing versus his essence, his true self, his uncertainty and innocence, the struggle to understand and control a changing body, changing hormones. He'd never be able to answer the questions that had probably kept him up nights, never be able to construct his identity this way or that.

"There's no problem," Toya said to Folami. "But there's also no plan." She looked at Folami and Fishbone. She glanced at Kanaan, who finally abandoned the pictures on the screen. He sat silently in the chair, his head in his hands, his dreads a curtain that hid his face in shadow.

"Plan?" Fishbone said. "The plan is to go." He swung his long arms at his side. "That's all the plan I need, ya'heard me? I stay ready to ride."

"What do we need to plan?" Folami screwed her face. Her eyes didn't search for answers to her question but seemed to challenge Toya to try to find one. "The news is clear. It's only like an hour drive," she said. "Dr. Abasi is already in Orlando, so he'll be there soon I'm sure."

"I just think we need a purpose. An agenda. Are we going to just be there? Are we going to sit outside the courthouse or mob up the police station? Do we want to try to contact the family? Are we staying overnight or coming back?" Toya didn't mean to assault Folami and Fishbone with questions, but she knew focus would make their presence more effective, more incendiary to the powers that be. Folami crossed her arms against her chest and flexed her jaw. Toya didn't balk. She challenged Folami because she wanted her to think their next move through, to step up like they had just talked about at the restaurant. It was time to respond not just react.

"You're stalling. You just promised to help me—I mean help us—and now you're stalling. If you don't want to work with RiseUP! no one is forcing you," Folami said.

"I didn't say that!" Toya said. "How could you say that I don't want to be there at all?"

"Look, Toya," Folami said. "I get it. I do. You aren't sure what you want to do. But I can't let your indecision hold us up." She swiped a stack of flyers off the table and slid them into her bag.

"Not sure? What are you talking about? Did you hear anything I said at the restaurant?" Toya's throat strained in frustration. Folami wouldn't look at her. She shifted things around in her bag. Her hands moved fast and hard, her body language accusatory and angry for reasons Toya struggled to put together. Was she upset because she wasn't following along blindly? Is that what Folami meant when she said she needed them to work together? Automatic cosigning and instant acquiescence? Or had the weight of their "breakup" finally settled on her shoulders?

"We can't and won't wait for you," Folami said. She nudged her chin to Fishbone and shot a quick look at Kanaan, who still hadn't moved from his seat, still hadn't released his temples.

Fishbone stuffed his hands in his pockets. "Like I said, I'm ready."

"Either you're with us or you're not, Toya," Folami said. Her voice sharp and cold. "There is no in—"

"Hold it right there!" Toya said. "Just a couple hours ago, I told you I was here. I'm here and I'm ready to do this work." She stood up. "I don't know where this is coming from, but you ain't right." She knew Folami was upset and frustrated, enraged and hurting, but she was severely misdirecting her emotions.

"Fuck are y'all talking 'bout?" Kanaan said. He raised his head and dropped his arms to his side as he slouched in his seat. "Whatever the hell y'all talking about don't matter right now. Don't nothing matter but mobilizing." He twisted his lips and returned his attention to the television screen. He pointed at the press conference footage, playing for at least the fifth time since they'd agreed to meet at the center. "That's the only thing we need to be talking about right now."

"That's what I'm saying," Folami said. She snapped her bag closed and slid in onto her shoulder. "Let's go."

Kanaan shook his head. "Nah," he said. He stood up slowly, his eyes never leaving the screen. Mr. Miles at the podium, his wife at his side, flashing lights and hands thrusting recorders and microphones in his direction. "We need to know what we're doing when we go up there. This is an opportunity," he said.

Toya raised an eyebrow, surprised that Kanaan actually agreed with her.

Folami plopped her bag on the table. "Are you serious?" She sighed long and loud. Her obvious irritation with Toya growing to include Kanaan, and maybe even Fishbone since he had yet to really move toward the door.

"Yes," Kanaan said. "The murder of that young brother is real. All this shit is real." He finally tore his eyes from the screen. "That's national coverage."

Toya nodded. "It's a large forum. The whole country is watching."

"We gotta come hard," Kanaan said. "We gotta come correct."

Toya and Kanaan met each other's eyes and shared a rare moment of accord. Toya gave him a small, appreciative smile. He smirked and shrugged, a gesture that acknowledged the oddity but necessity of their mutual point of view.

Folami flounced down into a chair. "Whatever," she said. "What do we do then?" She looked to Kanaan then to Toya.

Fishbone stepped closer to the table and grabbed a chair. He sat down, too. He pulled at the knot in the back of his bandana, pulling it tighter with a wince. "What we need?"

"We need numbers," Kanaan said. "Boots on the ground." He yanked his chair and moved to the table before sitting back down. He leaned forward and rested his elbows on his knees.

"The meeting tomorrow," Toya said. "We can use it to recruit people to make the trip with us." She envisioned a caravan of cars and trucks, the community riding out with passion and determination, road-tripping in solidarity. Everyone at the table nodded. Folami took a small notebook from her bag.

"Let's do this," she said.

The four of them talked all night. They made plans to shift the concentration of the general interest meeting to focus on the J'Quan Miles case. They shared ideas for presenting the facts, divvied up the research to learn all they could about the shooting, and assigned tasks for setting up the center and providing sign-up sheets to organize vehicles. They discussed their hopes for the meeting and for the movement overall, something larger and more powerful. Plans took shape and swelled between them as the sky lightened from black to navy blue streaked with pink and gold.

Chapter Seven

They nearly ran out of chairs. Men and women from the neighborhood, and even a few teenagers, filed into the center along with tentative, curious couples and energetic, expectant groups of three and four. Working people still in their work clothes—name tags and lanyards—came in exhausted but interested, and college students from South Florida University in dashikis and skinny jeans filed in smiling and eager to meet and mobilize.

"Come on in," Folami said. She and Fishbone worked as welcoming committee. Alternating their "Hey, brotha, good to see you"s and "Greetings, sis, you're in the right place"s as the living room and dining room filled to capacity. Some of the people knew each other; others made acquaintance as they negotiated for seats and places to stand. A pleasant hum of voices rose up alongside the assertive drums and Gil Scott Heron's sturdy, sentient tenor in song and spoken word.

"Can I have your attention, please?" Toya said. She made her way from the kitchen, where she had just checked on the vegetarian chili and tempeh stir-fry. Folami had made a salad earlier, and Fishbone brought a red velvet cake compliments of his grandmother. Toya slid between small huddles of people surrounding the dining room table. She stopped at the archway between the dining room and living room.

"We're pleased you could make it tonight. We got a lot to talk about and a lot of information to hand out. We also need information from you…" Toya paused to make eye contact with a chatting group of teenagers who pointed at the posters on the walls and whispered between themselves. Caught in her stare, they stopped talking and dropped their hands to their sides. "We also need your help. We're going to feed you." She smiled. "But we hope you ain't just come for the food. We hope that you came to lend your support. That you're here because you want to be a part of this very important movement." Toya searched the room for Folami, Fishbone, and Kanaan. She only found Folami and Fishbone. They gave her a head nod and a raised fist.

"This movement ain't nothing without y'all. If you're tired of the same old problems in your neighborhood—poverty, crime, unemployment, racial profiling, run-down schools, and busted up houses and streets—then you gotta do something different. We all gotta do something different. We have to raise our voices. We have to get in some faces. We have to show the people of this city, this state, this country, that we are here and we have demands. We have needs! And we will not be ignored!" Toya surprised herself with her candor and cadence, the strength and agitation in her voice. Folami and Fishbone's smiling faces encouraged her. "If you're tired of being ignored, let me hear you say it. Say 'I'm tired of being ignored!'" Toya raised her fist as everyone in the room repeated after her. "I'm tired of being ignored! I'm tired of being ignored! I'm tired of being ignored!"

The chant went on, growing in volume and speed. The energy in the room undeniable. Toya pumped her fist and smiled at Folami, who took over the lead.

"Black lives matter," Folami said. "Black lives matter," she repeated, clear and matter-of-fact. The crowd quieted, nodding agreement and leaning in. "This is our platform," she said, "Black lives matter." A few people applauded. Some people chimed in with "Word" and "That's right." Folami held up the one-page flyer she and Toya designed.

"It's not just a belief," Folami said. She looked at Toya then back out at the crowd. "It's at the core of our survival."

"Black lives matter!" Fishbone said, pumping his fist. The people in attendance joined in. "Black lives matter! Black lives matter!" he said, establishing a rhythm for the chant.

The energy in the room was so high, Toya barely noticed Kanaan standing at the front door. Dressed in all black, a sharp crease in his Dickies and a simple V neck T-shirt, Kanaan held the door open partway, watching the meeting rather than joining in. Toya waved him inside. He smirked then entered the living room. He looked around, his face unable to hide the surprise and appreciation the enthusiastic crowd evoked. He folded his arms and surveyed the room.

Toya held up a hand and the chanting quieted. "We got important information to hand out to you all. Details about the Black Lives Matter movement and the J'Quan Miles case." She gestured to Folami and Fishbone to start handing out the flyers.

The informational sheets, printed in simple, no-frills black-and-white, had a short overview of the Black Lives Matter movement. Quick bios for the founders, Alicia Garza, who coined the phrase in a social media post following the acquittal of a neighborhood watch member who shot and killed a young Black boy in a style all too similar to J'Quan Miles; Patrisse Cullors, who turned the phrase into a rallying cry; and Opal Tometi, who took the media movement of Black Lives Matter to the next level. The hope was that the people in attendance would see how far passion and energy could take them, how perfect the moment for mobilizing, and maybe even show them a new face of activism; the latter a sticking point for Toya when she made the flyer. The entire bottom half was a bullet-pointed list of all the J'Quan Miles details as they knew them, a small and grainy black-and-white rendering of Miles in the bottom corner.

"After you read through them, think about what YOU can do to help. To start, you can sign up to ride out to Evergreen with us tomorrow morning," Folami said as she passed out the papers to eager, reaching hands.

"We have a sign-up sheet floating around where you can put your name, number, and whether you want to ride or drive," Toya said.

Kanaan stood near the door, his arms folded across his chest as he nodded his approval. He forced a half-smile at Toya and shrugged. He whispered in Fishbone's ear and clapped him on the back.

Fishbone smiled then pushed through a small group of women near the closed door to Abasi's office. He cleared his throat and held up his hand for people's attention.

"Brother Kanaan just told me there's a rally tomorrow. They calling it 'Peace Rally for J'Quan.' If you was on the fence about riding out with us tomorrow, get yo' mind right. We gotta represent!" He shook his dreads and lifted his fist. He bounced on his toes then launched into a poem, the tempo quick and staccato, Toya would bet he was freestyling. People called for flyers and asked for the sign-up sheet while Fishbone mumbled through his verses, almost as if performing for himself. But when he began rapid-fire recitation of all the names of unarmed people murdered by police in the last year, everyone went silent and just listened.

❖

Folami, Fishbone, and Kanaan passed a blunt between them while Toya sipped on cheap merlot from a red plastic cup. She sipped the wine slowly, the tart, acidic bite sharper than Toya usually enjoyed in her red wine. She remembered her high school graduation and her mother insisting on opening a bottle of Screaming Eagle Cabernet. She took a deep swallow to chase away thoughts of her parents. She had been doing well not to think of them. Maybe her equilibrium was fucked up, too.

They sat in the semi-quiet of the night, the neighborhood sounds of laughter, a distant argument, and rumbling bass surrounding them in the small cement slab behind the center.

"I was surprised you didn't want to say anything, Kanaan," Fishbone said, taking a drag of the white grape cigarillo, the sweet aroma of the fruit mixing with the pungent citrus and flower smell of the weed. He passed the cigar to Kanaan, who stared at the glowing red cherry before taking it to his lips. He took a double pull and held the blunt between his index finger and thumb.

"To be honest, I didn't really have anything to say." Kanaan shrugged as he exhaled. The thick gray smoke curled over his top lip, and he pulled the smoke into his nose before blowing it out again. "I mean, y'all really had everything covered."

"Kanaan passing up a chance to talk? Today is definitely one for the books," Folami said. She took the blunt from Kanaan and took a small pull before handing it to Fishbone. He screwed his face at her tiny puff, but she jutted the cigar toward him with a shimmy of her shoulders. She didn't smoke often, and when she did, it didn't take much to get her at a comfortable high. "I never buy weed. If I smoke too much I get all paranoid and shit," she had told Toya one evening after Fishbone gave her a small nickel bag.

"I just don't like being out of control," Toya had said back then, passing on taking a toke from the psychedelic glass pipe Folami kept in a small velveteen pouch in her desk drawer.

"Nah, on the real, I didn't have anything to add. The info sheets came out just like y'all wanted. The crowd was…" Kanaan stared up at the sky as if reading the stars for the right word. "The crowd was diverse."

"Diverse?" Fishbone repeated. He sniggered. "That corporate ass word. What the fuck you mean 'diverse'?" He laughed from deep down, holding his stomach as his cackling became a cough. Folami laughed too, her giggling getting louder the more Fishbone coughed.

"There were some new faces in there. They seemed well meaning. Only a few of our regulars were there, which was a little disappointing, but the new faces was a good look," Kanaan said as Fishbone cleared his throat and caught his breath. He handed the blunt to Kanaan. "I figured I'd just let y'all engage," Kanaan said before taking a pull. He held the blunt out to Folami. She held up her hand to pass.

"I am done!" Folami said. "And I'm going to need some water. Anybody else?" Everyone shook their head, so she pushed herself up from the plastic yard chair and went into the house.

"Y'all were straight," Kanaan said with a smirk. "Weren't y'all?" He took a long puff and shot a mischievous grin to Fishbone, who put his hand over his mouth to stifle a laugh.

Toya drank from her cup to give herself a moment before responding. Kanaan, as usual, was trying to bait her. He stared at her, waiting.

"I don't think you know much about the movement," she said. "Maybe if we were talking about something you knew more about, you would have been more vocal." She sipped her wine and looked Kanaan in the eye. The meeting had been a success, the new faces were many—all of them interested in the movement, most of them wanting more information about the sheet. There weren't as many sign-ups for the rally as they would've liked, but the mood was hopeful.

Kanaan cut his eyes and stared at Toya through the smoke that rose like thick gauze across his face. "What?" he said.

"The Black Lives Matter movement. I don't think you know anything about it. It was the focal point of our flyer, along with the Miles information. You nodded along with me and Folami when we talked about it last night, but didn't have anything to add when we started planning the summary." Toya held her cup to her lips. Still high off the night, taking center stage had given her a bit of a buzz, and feeling the growing but subtle tingle of her wine, she didn't back down. For the first time in a long time, Toya didn't feel like she was on the sidelines, and she liked it. She was facing Kanaan, and in her mind, everyone like him, and she wouldn't back down. "So, I'm just saying that being a little out of your element tonight contributed to you not speaking. You didn't have anything to add. Literally."

"Fuck outta here," Kanaan said. "You don't know what the fuck I know. I know about that social media bullshit, and it ain't shit. Where the soldiers at?" He handed the blunt to Fishbone and rubbed his hands on his black jeans.

"Soldiers?" Toya said. "You trying to say the people behind this movement ain't soldiers? How the fuck you figure? If you think they just sitting around posting statuses and updating blogs, you really don't know shit." She shook her head and put her cup down on the wooden table beside her chair.

Kanaan nodded. "I'll admit it. They got some work. Ferguson was that boss shit." He dug around in his pocket for his cell phone. He swiped his screen and made a call. He held the phone to his face and looked at Toya. "I ain't trying to start no shit tonight, Toya. Tonight was good. For real. I got to give it up."

Toya didn't know what to say. If the wine was any good and she'd had more of it, she'd think she was drunk and hearing things. Perhaps Folami was right. It was simple. The struggle is all, and she'd be able to find her place if she'd just assert herself and come out of the fringes.

"Fish, I'm getting us a ride," Kanaan said. He mumbled into the phone as he walked toward the side of the house. Fishbone smoked the last of the blunt and smashed the tiny butt on the edge of his Converse.

"If his girl don't come, could you or Folami run us home?" Fishbone dropped the butt in the front pocket of his short-sleeved button up. He looked over at the RiseUP! community car, reserved for official center business, then looked over Toya's shoulder as Kanaan disappeared to the front of the house.

"I guess so," Toya said. "I haven't had that much to drink."

"Cool." Fishbone stretched and smiled at Folami as she came out the back door.

"I know you want some more of this wine, Toya," she said. She gripped the more than half-full bottle by the neck with one hand and held a large plastic tumbler of water in the other. She thrust the bottle in Toya's direction.

"Fish!" Kanaan called from the darkness. The low bump of bass grew louder and louder in front of the house. "FISH!"

"I guess she came," Fishbone said. "Surprised the hell out of me." He smiled and shrugged. He gave out loose, good-natured hugs to Folami and Toya before cutting through the shadows clinging to the side of the house.

"Guess you can have more wine," Folami said. She picked up the bottle from the card table and motioned for Toya to pass her cup.

"Not too much," Toya said, handing the cup over.

Folami poured fast, sliding back from Toya's reach as she filled the cup nearly to the top.

"That's too much," Toya said. She stood up and grabbed at her cup. Folami held it out of reach.

"You deserve a celebratory drink, Toya," Folami said. She put the bottle on the table and took a sip of the wine before handing it to Toya. "That shit is gross." She laughed.

"Yeah, it's not the best," Toya said. She sipped from the cup then put it down.

"You were amazing today," Folami said. She ran a hand through her afro and bit her lip. "I was...I was really blown away. I don't think I've ever heard you speak before. I mean, in front of a group." She looked down at her hands then raised her eyes to meet Toya's.

"I surprised myself," Toya said. "I was just feeling it, you know? This is exactly what I needed. Looking out at the faces, especially the new ones. All of us there for the same thing, feeling the same thing. I felt so…I felt so connected!"

"You and your feelings," Folami said. A slow grin danced across her full lips. She looked down at her hands.

Toya watched her. She seemed nervous, but maybe she was just high. "So you gonna give me grief about my feelings, huh?" she said with a laugh.

Folami nodded, finally returning her gaze to Toya. They stared into each other's eyes. There was no breeze. There was barely any light; the streetlamp in the alley gave the faintest orange glow to the backyard, and the light coming from the back door spilled down onto the small patch of grass. The scene was peaceful, nice.

"There is no way for me to separate my emotions from my sense of justice. This isn't business. And it isn't just political. It's personal. It's so very personal. I feel it in here," Toya said, putting a hand over her heart.

Folami put her hand on top of Toya's. She held it there and leaned in close. Her lips parted, she hesitated. Her eyes searched Toya's face. Toya took a deep breath, every part of her stiff and uncomfortable. She held herself that way, hard and cold, trying not to melt, trying to be stone not ice.

Folami closed the space between them, her lips soft and warm and beautiful and magic. Toya tightened her lips as Folami tried to slide her tongue between them. Toya took a step back.

"Don't," Toya said.

"Don't?" Folami said.

"I told you," Toya spoke slowly. She clenched her fists as if it would help steady her voice. Everything in her screamed to stop thinking, to stop making excuses. "I don't want you unless I can really have you," she said. Her body ached with the effort.

"You don't want me," Folami said. No trace of inflection or emotion. The sentiment sounded harder, heavier, almost hateful when she said it.

Toya wanted to take back what she'd said. She didn't mean it, but she had to say it. She couldn't go back, not after the night she'd had, not after finally standing up, being heard.

"No," Toya said. "I don't want this. I don't want you. I'm finally feeling like I can be part of something, and sneaking around with you…" She sighed and blinked back tears. "Tonight was a good night. Don't…don't ruin it."

Folami's eyes blazed with hurt. Tears came, but words did not. The silence too much to bear, Toya almost reneged on her own sentiment. Instead, she dropped her head to avoid Folami's eyes and bid her good night. When she got to the back door of the house, she stopped.

"You should take the car home. It's late," Toya said over her shoulder. She opened the back screen door and went inside the house.

BOOK III

Chapter Eight

"Hello?"

Toya pushed open the front door of the center. When it was empty, it was easier to see that the place was a converted house. The front rooms spacious with just a sofa and arm chair, a long wooden dining table with folding chairs. The walls lined with bookshelves, framed posters of Garvey and Ture, Karenga and Malcolm X. A large red, black, and green flag hung above the fireplace, African statuettes and wooden giraffes and lions stood side-by-side on the mantle.

"Anyone here?" Toya stepped fully inside, closing the door with a creak behind her. The office was dark, quiet, more peaceful than it had been in days. She walked toward the kitchen, the smell of copal and sage leading the way.

Folami sat on a stool near the sink. A cone of incense smoldering next to a half-filled glass of water. She glanced up at Toya from her newspaper then turned the page. Her auburn afro caught the sunlight from the large windows, the brightness a contrast to her face. Folami looked tired and irritated. She concentrated on the paper in front of her, and Toya stared at her forehead, the crinkle of skin between her eyebrows. She frowned as she read. They hadn't spoken since the night before, and while Toya thought it best that she call before showing up at the center, she suspected Folami wouldn't have answered. Toya tried to relax. She needed to stick to her choice, but seeing Folami in the bright of the morning, even with exhaustion heavy in her eyes, struck something in Toya. She took a deep breath and steadied herself. She had to be ready for anything. More angry shouting about J'Quan Miles and even the silent treatment from Folami.

"I didn't think anyone was here," Toya said.

Folami shrugged and didn't look up from her paper. The refrigerator hummed.

Toya leaned against the doorway and looked around the room. The counter was clean, all the glasses, bowls, and spoons from the night before washed and draining. The large stainless steel stew pot, previously brimming with vegetarian chili, sat gleaming on the stove alongside a drying cast iron skillet that had been used to fry tempeh.

"You cleaned the kitchen," she said. Toya stepped forward and grabbed a stool. Even though the sun blasted through the thin white curtains and the surface of the vinyl stool was warm against her palm, everything about the moment was cold. Folami was cold. And it was Toya's fault.

"It wasn't going to clean itself," Folami said.

"She speaks," Toya said with a nervous chuckle. "Why didn't you call me to come earlier? I would have helped."

Folami looked up and pursed her lips. She shook her head and looked back down at the paper. "You look like shit," she said.

"Red wine," Toya said.

"Cheap red wine," she said. She didn't look up from the paper.

"True. Plus, I didn't sleep last night," Toya said. She sat down and smoothed her hands over her thighs, the denim of her jeans already warming in the sunlight. "At all. I didn't sleep at all."

Folami nodded. "Me neither."

"You want to talk about it?" Toya said. She emptied her heart, tried to make it a cavern of nothingness so she wouldn't go back to caring too much, being too much in love.

"I don't even know where to begin," she said. She folded the paper, flipping the inside pages outside. She folded it again and jutted it forward.

Toya took the paper and stared down at the headline. Evergreen Prepares for J'Quan Miles Rally. Below the headline, police, dressed in black fatigues with helmets and clear shields, stood in perfect lines, rubber batons poised, an infantry ready for war.

"Can you believe that shit? Riot gear." Folami hopped off the stool. She grabbed her water and drank it down.

Toya read the article. The city claimed preparation for the worst-case scenario, the unruly and violent reactions of people frustrated and angry. The confusion, the article went on to say, stemmed from the murky details and contradictory accounts of what happened on a rainy night two weeks ago, when seventeen-year-old J'Quan Miles was shot in the chest, shoulder, and head by off-duty police officer Eric Vaughn. She read the call-out box near the fold, accompanied by a picture of J'Quan, scowling for the camera, imitation gold fronts along his bottom row of teeth and white tank top askew on his bony shoulders.

"Miles, seventeen, fatally shot by Deputy Eric Vaughn during suspected robbery." Toya clenched her fists on the edges of the paper.

"And don't even get me started on that shit," Folami said. "Suspected robbery," she repeated with a sigh. "Unbelievable."

Toya folded the paper lengthwise and tossed it on the table. She didn't know what to say. She looked down at her jeans, black T-shirt, and wood-beaded necklace. She clasped her hands around the large wooden Africa pendant that rested between her breasts. She liked the way it fit in her palm, her fingers curled around the coastlines. She closed her eyes and imagined watching the sunset on a beach, not a Florida beach, but one much, much farther away, miles and miles away from denying her feelings for Folami and anger about J'Quan's murder, a whole ocean away from the underwhelming offer of part-time, undercover love and unarmed teens murdered on neighborhood streets. The sun coming through the kitchen windows and landing on her face transported her in that brief moment, and Toya saw the sun setting across the sands of Beyin. She could hear it sizzling as it dipped into the Atlantic.

"Are you going to say anything?" Folami said.

Toya opened her eyes. "I don't know what you want me to say." She stared down at her pendant.

Folami pushed herself from the counter and put her hands on her wide hips. "Are you fucking with me?"

Toya started to speak then stopped. Was she talking about the newspaper and the riot gear or last night? She frowned.

"No. I'm not fucking with you. I just don't know what you want me to say." Toya released her Africa pendant and pressed her hand on the paper. "This," Toya said, standing up slowly, "is fucked up." She hesitated before continuing, "And this"—she gestured at the space between them—"is fucked up, too."

Folami rolled her eyes.

"It's just that we have a lot of work to do, but I want to be sure we can do what we need to, without it being weird. And awkward." Toya sighed and looked out the window.

"I wasn't even talking about...that...about last night. I'm trying not to talk about it at all if you hadn't noticed," Folami said.

"I did notice. I just want to make sure we're okay."

"Well, you made yourself perfectly clear," Folami said. She turned and faced the sink. Her back to Toya, she continued, "You're right about focusing on the movement. We're done. I get it. It's fine. Let's not make it a whole thing." She shook her head and waved her fingers, dismissing the entire ordeal in a fluttering blur of slender fingers and shiny, bright red nails.

Toya's heart, the cave she struggled to make of it, collapsed, the jagged rocks and dusty crumbles of stone making her cough. She cleared her throat then coughed again. Folami finally looked at her, twisting her head over her shoulder.

"You want some water?" Folami said. She returned to the sink and filled her empty glass with water from the faucet. She took another deep breath. "Seriously, Toya. Let's just move on from it. Fuck all these feelings and focus on the work." She stood at the sink and glanced at Toya over her shoulder again. "It's like Director Abasi says, emotion makes us do things we otherwise would not." She turned back to the sink and shut off the water. "Emotion is the enemy of logic, the destroyer of reason."

Toya hated when Folami quoted the Director Abasi, who warned them all of becoming taken by emotion, or letting feelings overpower a solid sense of reason. He said women, in particular, had to work harder at being in control of themselves and their emotions if they planned to be useful and effective in the struggle. After he said it, Folami and Toya had shared a look, or at least Toya thought they had. An incredulous look. A look that called bullshit. Looking at Folami in that moment, accepting the rejection wholly, and supporting it with that anti-emotion wackness, disappointed Toya in the worst way.

Folami handed Toya the glass of water. "I mean it's, you know, nothing for us to dwell on. Just...let's just..." She swallowed and took a deep breath before squaring her jaw. "It's nothing," she repeated. She exhaled like she had been trapped underwater.

Toya searched Folami's face, lingering at her eyes, trying to see if she were trying to say something more than her lips were saying, hunting for that something that made her eyes fill with tears the night before. Folami's beauty ever present, her passion without question, Toya thought she saw something. Something pulsing like stars—explosive but so, so far away. Damn reason and logic and everything Folami had just said. Toya wanted to take it back. She wanted to take it all back and take her right on the kitchen table, the sunlight their spotlight, Toya wanted to take Folami in front of the window, unashamed, wild, and free.

"So, we're cool, right?" Folami smiled a crooked smile meant to reassure.

Toya drank the water, killed it in loud gulps. "Yeah," she said. Emotion is the enemy of reason. She put the glass on the table, smiled, and shrugged, considering, and not for the first time, that she might have been projecting. Maybe Folami was not in love with her. Perhaps she didn't feel what Toya felt. And even though it was Toya who cut everything off, she grieved their love, in all its dysfunction.

"Yeah?" Folami said.

"Yeah. We're cool."

"Good." Folami sighed. "So, about the muthafuckin' riot gear."

"Complete overkill," Toya said. She rubbed her throat then cleared it again.

"Complete bullshit!" Folami swiped the paper off the table. She opened it to the story, shaking her head. "It's like we're always talking about it. Shit ain't changed. From inception, the police state ain't been about shit but busting our heads under the guise of law and order!"

"Say that shit, sis!" a voice yelled from the front room.

Folami and Toya looked at each other. They left the kitchen and stood just inside the dining room area. "Hotep, Queens." Kanaan said, a little smirk playing at the corner of his mouth.

"What's up, Kanaan?" Toya said.

"Hey, Kanaan," Folami said. She walked to meet him in the front room then held the paper out to him. "You see this shit?"

Kanaan took off his sunglasses and hooked them to the collar of his black Garvey T-shirt. He stared down at the paper. He shook his head. "They right," he said. "They best be prepared. We need our soldiers to be prepared too!" He put his sunglasses back on. "Matter fact, I'm waiting on a few brothas to call me back within the hour to help us do just that."

"Help us do what?" Toya asked.

"Get prepared," Kanaan said.

"Preparation is not the point," Folami said. "I'm as furious as the next person, but the J'Quan Miles rally was announced as a peace rally. A peace rally for justice. His parents are gonna be there. Kids and families. Vendors and performers. They know that shit, and they respond with riot gear?"

"Folami's right," Toya said. "Most Black people don't even walk around carrying weapons, let alone congregating with weapons. Shit, we go to rallies prepared to get arrested. Hoping to sometimes." She grabbed a folding chair and sat in front of a bookshelf stocked with an *Encyclopedia Britannica* and an entire shelf of National Geographic photography collections. The collection grabbed her the moment she had stepped into the RiseUP! Center for her first meeting a little over a year ago. Being near it reminded her of that day. A good day, something like a fresh start. She needed that kind of energy again.

"And that's the problem," Kanaan said. "Black people organize to get arrested. We should be organizing our fellow Afrikans to fight back."

Toya sighed and looked at Folami, who took the paper from Kanaan and read the headline again. "They don't even mention it as a peace rally for justice. Not once," she said.

"They don't care," Kanaan said. "So we shouldn't care either."

"And let the bodies pile up?" Toya said.

Kanaan raised his hand as if in worship and said in a singsong sermon voice, "Until the stink rises up to heaven and upsets the almighty Jesus on his throne!"

CHAPTER NINE

The ride to Evergreen started out lively. The mumbles, shouts, and sighs of healthy, thoughtful, passionate debate filled the car. Folami, Kanaan, Fishbone, and Toya rode with the windows down, the swoosh of humid Florida air inflating their words as they inflated their chests. At one point, they were all speaking at once and only snatches of words—criminal, ridiculous, power, Black, community, African, America, White supremacy, patriarchy, capitalism, colonialists—made it through the rumbling engine of the 2001 Impala that served as the community car used for official RiseUP! business.

"Don't pigs supposed to fire warning shots or something?"

"But that's what I'm saying, Fish," Kanaan said. "It's like target practice for these pigs. They do this shit for sport!"

"And he was off-duty," Folami said. She leaned forward and rested her elbows on either side of the headrests. The fact being stated for the second time since they'd started talking.

"Exactly! That's what I'm saying, Queen! Fuckin' sport!" Kanaan said, slamming his hands on the steering wheel.

"Rekia Boyd was killed by an off-duty cop, too," Toya said. She sat back, offering an example for the last point she had made about unnecessarily gendering police brutality.

"Exactly," Folami said. "What was the cop even doing in Rekia's neighborhood off-duty?"

"I asked the same thing," Toya said.

The men were suddenly silent. Folami saved them both, giving an overview of the case before bringing them back to the topic in general: use of deadly force. The conversation led them back, once again, to the endangered Black man, and soon only Kanaan's booming voice could be heard through the wind.

"That's why it's time. The brothas that stopped by before we left? They know what's up. They coming up later this afternoon. Real soldiers. Watch the hunters become the prey in this bitch! The Afrikan man ain't nobody's sport," Kanaan said.

"Who are these dudes?" Toya asked. She looked at Folami for support. Kanaan and a group of men had huddled on the porch and spoke in whispers while she and Folami gathered the camera equipment. By the time they made it outside to load the car, the men had already gone, an indistinguishable collection of snapbacks, oversized white tees, and baggy jeans. They each had red, black, and green bandanas hanging out of their back pockets.

"They're friends of mine. And they ready. That's all you need to know," Kanaan said.

Toya sighed and looked out the window. She knew Kanaan wouldn't divulge anything useful. She would have to ask Fishbone about it later, maybe once they got to the park and separated to explore.

"I say something you don't like?" Kanaan said. He pulled the car off the highway and slowed on the ramp. His head tilted up toward the rearview. Toya couldn't see his eyes through the damn mirrored sunglasses.

"You already know how I feel," Toya said. "I'm nonviolent. I don't want to deliberately hurt people. And I find it curious that you get so riled up about the murder of Black men but act like Black women ain't filling up morgues right alongside them."

Folami sat back. "She right, Kanaan. We all in this fight together."

"First," Kanaan said, turning into a gas station. He parked the car at a pump near the exit then twisted in his seat to look at Toya.

"I said 'Afrikan' not 'Black.'" He looked at Fishbone, who rolled one of his fat, knotty dreads between his fingers and nodded.

"Second, you can bring up all the cases of Afrikan women being murdered you want; at the end of the day, the majority of this heinous shit is coming down on our heads. The number of cases of pig brutality against Afrikan men is way higher than that of Afrikan women. And third," he said. He turned the car off and slid the key out of the ignition. "That Kumbaya shit is played. What the fuck has marching and rallies and boycotts and sit-ins done for us lately? Not a goddamn thing. There was a time we could hold hands and hold signs and shit, but do you see what's happening? They killing us and leaving us to die in the fuckin' street! They don't give a fuck about capping our ass. So why should we just sit idly by and let them do it? You can save that 'turn the other cheek' shit for some other muthafucka! It's time to do more than chant! It's time to spill some of they blood in the street!" He said the last with so much venom his sunglasses fell off his face. His burnt umber eyes blazed as he caught his breath. He picked up his glasses from the center armrest, then jumped out of the car so quickly it bounced.

Folami, Fishbone, and Toya sat in silence. They looked at one another with raised eyebrows. Toya took a deep breath then got out of the car. She needed some air. She walked around the back of the car and leaned against the trunk. She saw Kanaan coming out of the gas station, so she decided to go in. She dipped her head to the back window.

"Anybody want anything? Water or something? We should get it now because I don't want to give Evergreen a penny of my money," Toya said.

"I'm good," Fishbone said. He rolled at the end of another dread.

"I'll take a water," Folami said.

Toya nodded then stood up. Kanaan started pumping the gas. He looked at Toya over the top of the car, and Toya returned his stare.

"How would you know?" Toya asked.

"How would I know what?" Kanaan said. He squared his shoulders then settled back on his heels.

"About the number of cases. Black men being killed more than Black women. There's no way to know really. No one talks about them. They rarely make the news. No one rallies for them." Toya crossed her arms.

"You're reaching," Kanaan said. He stared back at me. The sun glinted off his silver frames. He put his chew stick in his mouth and grinned.

"Not at all," Toya said. "Not even two hundred people showed up for the rally for Rekia Boyd. Hell, I'm not even sure one hundred people showed up." She frowned, a knot of sorrow and rage settling in her gut.

"Did you go?" Kanaan said with a smirk.

"I wish I had," Toya said. "I really wish I had. But you and I both know that isn't the point."

"I get your point." Kanaan took his chew stick out of his mouth. "But you can miss me with your feminist rhetoric. I know that racket. It's divisive."

"How is pressing you to include Black women in your rants about oppression and police brutality divisive? If anything, it's more inclusive. This is the bullsh—"

"Whoa!" Kanaan reeled back. "When the fuck did you get so vocal?" He chuckled. "You been jumping real hard these last few days. A whole year of you standing around taking pictures and following behind Folami, and now…" Kanaan's eyes widened. He smiled, slow and sly, a cat with canary feathers stuck in his teeth.

"What?" Toya looked over her shoulders self-consciously and smoothed the front of her T-shirt, "Danger Educated Negro" screen-printed across her small breasts.

"I just figured it out." Kanaan smirked. "Folami gave you a whiff and now you think you bad," he said.

"What the fuck did you just say to me?" Toya took two long, heavy strides toward Kanaan, who held a hand up as he pulled the gas pump out partway.

"Hey, hey!" he said.

Folami jumped out of the car and ran up to Toya. "Yo, be cool, y'all." She grabbed Toya's arm and pulled her away from Kanaan.

"You ain't hear what this muthafucka just said!" Toya yelled.

"Cool it!" Folami said. "It doesn't matter. Just cool it!"

Toya shrugged Folami's hands off her and dropped her shoulders in defeat. "Are you serious right now?" She looked from Folami to Kanaan and back again. Folami glanced at Kanaan, who shrugged and held his hands up innocently.

"Fuck it," Toya said. She walked to the convenience store and went inside. She hated that she let Kanaan get under her skin, and the comment about Folami was uncalled for and way off base. It was actually getting out from under Folami that had fueled her bravado. She hadn't really thought of it as all connected in that way before, yet Toya couldn't deny that pulling away from Folami had actually brought her closer to understanding her role in the movement. She didn't know exactly what she needed to do to be most effective, but she was on the precipice; she needed only to open herself up. She yearned to fully embrace everything she felt and secretly hoped that the rally would unlock that final piece. It was time. Had been time.

Toya returned from inside the station with three waters and a bag of plantain chips. Kanaan sat in the car and Fishbone cleaned the windows. Folami had gotten out of the car, too, and stood against the back passenger door, scrolling through her phone.

"Stop letting Kanaan get to you," Folami said as Toya handed her a bottle of water.

"I'm trying," Toya said. She shrugged, placed the other two water bottles on the roof of the car, and squeezed at her bag of plantain chips. She felt Folami's eyes on her. They were kinder than they had been all day. Toya decided not to tell her what Kanaan had said. "He's ridiculous and you know it."

"He's a lot of things, but ridiculous isn't one of them. He has some good points, Toya." Folami slipped her phone into the back pocket of her shorts. "He gets excited. Maybe a bit too excited for some situations, but—"

"Why do you defend him?" Toya asked.

"What do you mean 'defend' him?" Folami walked around the back of the car. Fishbone finished the driver side window and moved on to the windshield. He mumbled under his breath, probably lines from one of his poems.

"Whenever I say something about him or dismiss one of his ideas or…it's just that you always take his side." Squinting against the sun, she pulled open the bag of plantains.

Folami furrowed her neat eyebrows and shook her head. "This ain't about sides, Toya." She sighed. "Can Kanaan be aggressive? Yes. Can Kanaan be abrasive? Yes. But it's only because he's so invested, so down for the struggle. I know where he's coming from. We live this thing."

"And I don't?" Toya asked, raising her voice. She glanced over at Fishbone. He looked at the both of them for a second then went over to dip the squeegee into the container near the trash can.

"Not really," Folami said. She pursed her lips to the side and put her hands on her hips. "We aren't like you. We don't come from money. We been poor and struggling through it all, our whole lives. We're here because we have to be. You're here because—" She stopped. Her arms dropped to her sides.

"Bringing up my parents is a low blow, Folami." Toya swallowed hard, forcing memory down and as far away as possible.

"Just forget it," Folami said. She threw her hands up and turned, headed back to the passenger side of the car.

"Yeah, just forget it." Toya shook her head. "You're obviously on bullshit now too."

"Hey, you're the one that told me about your parents," Folami said. She glanced down at her feet. Toya looked, too. Red painted toes, black flips. "And maybe now that we've…that we've parted, I can be more objective. You were so amped up last night. Maybe this is all some kind of high for you. Maybe you're just here because it's exciting." She shrugged as if it were all too obvious.

"Really, Folami?" Toya hated her for bringing her family up. She had struggled to make her parents understand that their neat little suburban Milwaukee life—manicured lawns and housekeepers, private schools and dinner parties—made her feel sheltered and ineffective rather than safe and encouraged. She told Folami about her parents in confidence, shared her confusion about her mother's message in a moment of intimacy vulnerability and here she was using it as a litmus test of her dedication to the struggle.

Growing up, the history of racial injustice was fed to her in bite-sized morsels, tales presented like folklore, easy to swallow factoids about separate water fountains and assigned bus seats. The moral of each story being "look how far we've come," the history of it all reduced to echoes as if her father's private practice and her mother's board seats nullified the realities of the here and now.

"You know damn well my family situation ain't got shit to do with what we're talking about," Toya said. "I'm down for this movement just as much as you, Fish, and Kanaan, and it's shitty for you to suggest otherwise."

Folami shot a glance at Fishbone as he made his way to the passenger side to get back in the car. "Whatever," she said.

"Yeah, whatever," Toya repeated.

They both returned to the car and sat as far away from each other as the backseat would allow.

Chapter Ten

Kanaan found a parking spot, a tight squeeze between a cluster of scooters and a conversion van. Folami, Toya, and Fishbone climbed out of the car before Kanaan even shifted the car into park.

"This is amazing," Folami said as Kanaan finally got out and joined them all beside the car. They walked toward the entrance of the park.

"There has to be over five hundred people here," Toya said, looking around. She hadn't known what to expect, but she hadn't quite expected so many people. Sure, the J'Quan Miles shooting had made national headlines, but she didn't think hundreds of people would show up and show out for the J'Quan Miles Peace Rally for Justice in Evergreen, Florida, a small, sweat-stain town right in the armpit of the peninsula. "It's beautiful," she said.

"This is exactly what you want to see," Fishbone said. He smiled and walked ahead. "This is how you show them what and who matters, y'all." He joined in with a group of women wearing matching airbrushed shirts, "RIP JQ" in blue and black bubble letters across their breasts.

Kanaan crossed his arms. "It's definitely a lot more people than I thought would show up." He looked around the park and up the crowded sidewalk where vendors had set up tables and booths. He nodded in approval. Then narrowed his eyes to survey the crowd once more.

Officers in uniforms, short-sleeved black shirts and black pants, their waists heavy with firearms and stun guns, stood cross-armed around the entrance and on random corners.

"No riot gear," Toya said. "I wonder why." She looked at Folami, who shrugged and kept walking.

"I don't," Kanaan said. He took off his shades. "They scared. And they should be."

"I don't know, Kanaan," Folami said. She glanced over her shoulder and nudged her chin toward an officer directing traffic away from an abandoned parking lot. "Maybe they know we aren't here for trouble. Maybe they thought better of their plans."

"Right. Pigs with conscience." Kanaan shook his head and rolled his eyes. "I'm gonna go find Director Abasi," he said. "Make sure your phones are on." He slid his sunglasses back on then jogged a little to catch up with Fishbone.

Folami and Toya stepped to the side to watch the scene, the lively, colorful mix of people pouring into the park from all sides. Church groups hopped out of long, tinted-windowed vans, with crosses and Bible verses screen-printed on T-shirts and jackets, which they wore dutifully, even in the early afternoon heat. A woman carrying two swaddled babies turned to encourage the collection of boys and girls, ages ranging from five to fifteen, to keep up and stay together. A man in army fatigue shorts and no shirt carried a boy, with an afro bigger than Folami's, on his shoulders. A small group of scraggly-looking white women with dreads, their tie-dyed shirts too big and their thin cotton midi skirts long and wrinkled, carried baskets of multicolored friendship bracelets and bright yellow flyers.

Folami nudged Toya as one of the women, the one with the basket, approached them. She held out the basket and Folami turned her head. Toya took a bracelet and nodded a thank you. The woman looked at Folami, but Folami refused to acknowledge her. The woman bowed, mumbled "Namaste" and walked away to join her friends.

"Really, Toya?" Folami said.

"What? Cause I took the bracelet?"

"It ain't about the bracelet," she said. She cut her eyes at the white women as they made their way through the vendors. "We just can't have nothing, can we? And here you go, encouraging them." She waited for a teenage couple, holding hands and carrying a banner that read "No Justice, No Peace" to pass before heading toward the sidewalk.

Toya inspected the bracelet. Its blue and white threads braided to hold five white beads, which were flat on one side with black letters, spelling out "peace." She jammed the bracelet in her pocket and jogged to catch up with Folami, her camera bag clunking against her hip.

They walked through the vendors who lined the sidewalk that ran alongside the park. Tables with tons of T-shirts, the faces of Martin Luther King Jr., Malcolm X, and Barack Obama folded just below the nose. Framed posters and prints of African kings and queens holding each other or holding up the earth lay against table legs and hung from makeshift walls. Handmade earrings and necklaces, beaded bracelets and adjustable cowrie shell rings, sat in neat rows among mix tapes, books, and DVDs. Toya recognized a lot of the titles, *Turn off the Radio*, *The Miseducation of the Negro*, and *Hidden Colors*, from the media collection at the RiseUP! Center.

Folami stopped at a vendor playing James Brown "I'm Black and I'm Proud" to admire his offering of blown up, framed photographs of the March on Washington, Rosa Parks sitting on a bus, and Tommie Smith and John Carlos at the '68 Olympics, fists raised and head bowed on the platform.

"I got that one," Toya said. She pointed at an enlarged photo of Fannie Lou Hamer speaking at Tougaloo College. The moment caught her holding the podium, her shoulders hunched and tight, hip slanted out to one side, and head tilted in exhaustion. "It's hanging in my living room."

"She looks tired," Folami said.

"I can't even imagine," Toya said, running her finger along the bottom of the plastic black frame.

"I'm sorry," Folami said. She looked at Fannie Lou Hamer then at Toya.

"For what?"

"What I said at the gas station." She shrugged. "I'm sorry. It's not you. I'm just...I'm buggin'."

"It's okay," Toya said.

"It's not okay. I don't know that I've been communicating very well. Half the time I'm walking around at a complete loss for words. I'm exhausted. I'm frustrated." Folami shrugged again, blinking back tears. "But I also feel restless, like I'm stuck or something. Like I need to do something. I just don't know what." Tears came then, poured down in quick, fat drops. She looked away and wiped her eyes. "See," she choked on the word. "I can't even stop myself from crying." She wiped at her face then looked away.

"I do know what you mean," Toya said. "I feel it, too. Last night was great, but not a single car showed up to ride out with us this morning."

"Exactly!" Folami said. Her eyes wide and wet. "There is an energy that we need to tap into, and I don't know how we do it. I don't know what else to do. I'm having a hard time being hopeful that anything will ever change."

"You can't lose your hope," Toya said. "It's what draws people to you. It's what drew me to you." She smiled and put her hand on Folami's shoulder. "Remember when we met?"

"Yes." Folami wiped at her eyes again.

Almost a year had passed since they met on that Wednesday afternoon. The heat of the day had been suffocating, the small flyer in Toya's hands nearly melting, the ink all but rubbed off by the sweat in her palms. The flyer put out a call to all concerned, conscious brothers and sisters who wanted to raise their voices in the community. RiseUP! printed in red block letters and OPEN FORUM in thick black script. Toya stood in front of the center but didn't know it. A dusty silver Impala pulled up and a short, shapely woman with an explosive auburn afro got out and walked around to the back of the car. Her face bright and inviting, she smiled at Toya as she opened the trunk.

"You look lost," Folami had said. She pushed the trunk up then wrestled a large blue plastic tub up and out, heaving it against her body. She tilted back, her face determined and shining with sweat, and rested the bin against her chest and thighs before slamming the trunk closed. The sight of her shimmering bronze skin and the booming reddish-brown of her afro's rebellious coils and curls, caught Toya quick. She stuffed the flyer in her front pocket in a rush to help her.

"Thanks," the woman said.

"No problem." Toya hesitated. She dug into her pocket and yanked out the flyer, tearing it a little in her haste and nervousness. "Uh…I'm looking for this address."

"You're in the right place." The woman nudged her chin forward toward the wooden shotgun house with peeling white paint.

Toya looked down at the flyer and then up at the woman who raised her eyebrows on the battered flyer.

"Maybe I should get the director to spring for card stock next time." She smiled. "I'm Folami."

"Toya."

Toya extended her hand, but Folami just looked at it before gently but firmly grabbing Toya's shoulders, her hands warm and strong. She pulled Toya into a tight, familiar, inviting hug.

"Now that was a good hug," she said with an approving nod and smile. "You smell good."

Toya had blushed. Actually blushed. She couldn't remember the last time someone made her face flush so hot and tingly.

"Thank you," she said.

"Sandalwood, yes?" Folami said.

"Yeah."

"Thought so," Folami said. "Smells like these incense I use at home."

Toya frowned, and Folami laughed, the sound gloriously warm and bright.

"Don't look like that. It's not an insult." She shrugged and bent to pick up the plastic bin. "You smell like home. That's a good sign."

For someone who hadn't thought of home or felt at home in a long while, the exchange filled Toya with a sense of hope and renewal. She remembered thinking, helping Folami carry the plastic bin into the center, that maybe, just maybe, she had found where she belonged.

"We're on to something," Toya said, leaving the memory of that Wednesday afternoon behind with a sigh. "I believe that."

"Yeah," Folami said. "I guess so. It just doesn't…"

"Being here in this moment is the only place for us to be right now. It's a calling. We gotta be open to it," Toya said, her hand still resting on Folami's shoulder.

"I'm trying. I'm tired, but I'm trying," Folami said, looking deep into Toya's eyes.

Toya felt strange comforting Folami. It seemed odd talking about an openness she hadn't quite embraced for herself. Meeting Folami's penetrating stare, she became certain that they were feeling the same thing, the same need. And not just for love, but for movement, for action, for something bigger and larger than the two of them. Hunger, Toya thought, can sometimes feel like exhaustion. She wanted to say that to Folami, but didn't.

Toya broke their eye contact and cleared her throat. She scanned the areas near the vendors and stopped when she spotted a small opening between a table stocked with shea butter, black soap, and oils and a cart of scarves, kufis, and dresses. She pointed. "There. Let's set up there."

"Sure," Folami said. "Let's do it."

Toya went into her shoulder bag and took out her camera, a black Nikon D3200, the best Christmas gift her parents ever gave her, and the last. After Toya had laid everything on the line, her politics, her dreams, her sexuality, her parents shut down and cut her off. "If that's the kind of lifestyle you've chosen, you can pay for it yourself," her father had said matter-of-factly. Her mother looked on, a quiet, convicting judge. Their last deposit to her account covered her rent for a while, and her savings account, currently on financial fumes, had kept her afloat while she focused on her photography, shooting for RiseUP! and taking other small gigs here and there. Toya didn't like thinking about them. Didn't like going back there, but every time she held the heft of the camera, curved her hands along the sides, and carefully attached the zoom lens, she balanced the memories of the enthusiastic support of what her parents had called a "worthy hobby" and the crushing indictment of what her parents had called an abomination unto God.

"You all right?" Folami asked.

"Yeah," Toya said. "I'm good." She moved to take the tripod out of the bag but stopped. She slipped her Nikon over her head, the thick strap kissing and holding the nape of her neck, the camera a familiar weight on her chest. She lifted the camera with both hands and put her eye to the viewer. She looked around the park, up and down the aisle of vendors, up at the sky, and down at the ground. She scanned the entire scene, opening herself up to receive the perfect shot.

A short, bald-headed boy wearing a LeBron James jersey and red shorts reached up to put his arm around a tall, lanky girl in a yellow and white sundress. Toya pressed the button, capturing the awkward, barely-reaching embrace. Two men greeted each other with solemn faces and handshakes; the darker skinned man pulled the lighter skinned man into a one-armed hug, and they shared a smile. Click.

A woman with a purple head wrap rearranged a mangled piece of tissue and dabbed at her face. Click.

A boy leaned his head against his mother's shoulder. She kissed him on the top of his head, pressed her mouth and nose through his high top fade. Click.

"You ready?" Folami said.

Toya snapped a few more shots then turned the camera to Folami.

Click.

Folami put her hands on her hips and smiled. Toya held the camera steady. Beauty. Unfiltered beauty.

Click.

A teasing smile curled the corners of Folami's full lips. "Let's start shooting," she said.

Toya set up the tripod and attached the camera. She positioned it on Folami, capturing both her and the main entrance of the park, Hillside in wrought iron letters across the top of the gate, and a few of the vendor tables.

"I think we're good," Toya said. She prepared the camera to record.

Kanaan walked up to Toya as she made last-minute adjustments. "Wait a second," he said. He started toward Folami, and Toya held up a hand to halt him. She nodded at Folami to begin. She zoomed in to frame Folami's face, to catch the fire in her eyes as she spoke directly into the camera.

"The case is simple. J'Quan Miles was murdered," she said. "And an off-duty officer stands guilty but uncharged."

Toya zoomed out, changing to a wide-angle shot as Folami announced the title, location, and time the rally was set to begin. Folami paused before she began the call to action, but before she could continue, Kanaan stepped directly into the shot.

"What are you doing?" Folami asked. She scrunched her face and glanced at Toya behind the camera. "Toya?"

Toya cut and lowered the camera.

Kanaan cleared his throat. "Director Abasi thinks I should speak on the video."

Folami and Toya frowned.

"What? Why? I do the videos," Folami said. She placed a hand on her chest. "I've done them from the beginning. They were my idea."

Kanaan took a deep breath and nodded. "I know, I know." He nodded some more. It was a paternal gesture. Parental even. He was handling her, talking to her like she was a whining child. Toya knew the technique, encountered it often in community meetings where certain voices were sidelined. The acknowledging of ideas, of feelings, of assertions, to ultimately ignore them.

"Director Abasi just thinks that I would be a better fit for this issue. That I would be a better face for this message," Kanaan said.

Toya put her hands on her hips. "What do you mean 'this message'? How is this message any different from the message we always share? The struggle, especially—"

"Look, LaToya," Kanaan interrupted. "There is a dynamic here that...a male dynamic that even though you think you know about it, you don't. Never will."

"Male dynamic? What the fuck are you talking about?" Toya said.

"Toya, chill," Folami said. "Just...just let it go."

Incredulous, Toya looked at her. "Let it go? Are you fucking kidding me?"

"Toya," Folami said. She pleaded peace with her eyes.

Toya shook her head. "Whatever," she said with a shrug. She adjusted the camera, directed Kanaan to step back, decided on a wide-angle to use throughout, and motioned to him when recording started.

He spoke passionately, a bit too quickly, but full of fervor, full of conviction. What he shared on camera was truth—the truth about racial profiling, the truth about fear, the truth about our history, the blood of it all old and dried and red in the center, and brown and black too, yellowed edges, layers of blood, stained on us, hard and crusted. Yet, even in all his passionate truth-telling, at no point did he say a single thing Folami couldn't have said, not a single thing she hadn't said already, in one form or another, at one forum or another. The observation irritated Toya all the more, and she fought the urge to stop the taping and tell him so as he brought his provocative but unpolished thoughts to a close. Toya cut and stepped back from the camera.

"How did I do?" Kanaan asked. He smirked in challenge and triumph.

"Okay," Toya said. "You need to work on delivery though. You were talking too fast. The speed makes you seem nervous."

"Nervous?" Kanaan raised an eyebrow.

"Yeah. Nervous." She took the camera off the tripod and returned it to her neck. "Were you nervous?"

"No," Kanaan said quickly. "I wasn't nervous." He raised his voice. "I wasn't nervous at all."

Fishbone walked over and stood between them. "Director Abasi wants us to get into the crowd. Find a good place to mix with the other protestors, maybe meet some people from Evergreen."

Kanaan and Toya still stared each other down. Folami sighed and shook her head. "Come on, Fishbone. Let's go." She hooked her arm through Fishbone's arm and pulled him away.

"I wasn't nervous," Kanaan said again.

"Well, you sounded like it," Toya said. She lifted her camera and focused on a vendor holding up a T-shirt with Tupac rendered as a pharaoh. She snapped the picture, Kanaan's eyes still on her. She ignored him and caught the exchange of money and T-shirt, the customer holding the shirt up against himself—it was going to be too big—and snapped his satisfied grin. Kanaan stared a second longer then pushed past her to catch up with Folami and Fishbone.

Chapter Eleven

Toya walked by herself through the crowds, taking a few shots and watching. People were talking with each other, meeting new people and even reconnecting. She overheard two women say they hadn't seen each other since they both left Evergreen eight years ago. They hugged then held each other's hands as they spoke. She snapped a picture of them both bowing their heads as if in prayer, their hands linked at the fingers. Toya weaved in and out of the crowd and settled on a spot to stay until the performances started.

A small group moved into the area where Toya stood scrolling through pictures in her camera. One of the men in the group, his face wrinkled and serious, set an Igloo cooler down and slid a canvas chair off his shoulder. He set that up, and the two younger men with him, their hair cut into matching faux hawks, situated their chairs beside him, one on each side. A woman with long gray dreads and a flowing purple dress steered a gaggle of toddlers in and around the man and the boys. A woman, slender with a Grace Jones cut and denim vest adorned with buttons and painted slogans like "Freedom NOW!" and "Love is the Answer" made room for herself close to Toya. She had a large sign, a wide poster board framed with red, black, and green colored duct tape, and a shoulder bag with a clipboard inside. She looked at Toya, dark eyes piercing, eyebrows neat, a silver stud in her nose. She gave a head nod before hoisting her sign up overhead.

"What Speed Should I Walk?" asserted itself in fat, hard, block letters, everything in black except for "Walk," which screamed loudest in bright red. She pumped the sign up and down, yelling, her voice loud but raspy, "BLACK LIVES MATTER! BLACK LIVES MATTER!"

The woman with the gray dreads, the men in their portable chairs, and the children joined in. "BLACK LIVES MATTER! BLACK LIVES MATTER!"

Toya picked up her camera and snapped a flurry of shots. The children pumping their fists, the two faux-hawked young men standing to pump their fists while holding up their sagging skinny jeans, and the old man, digging into his crate to pull out a bullhorn. He held it up to his mouth and joined in the chant.

"BLACK LIVES MATTER! BLACK LIVES MATTER!" he shouted into the microphone, the deep timbre of his voice shooting up and out. A few people turned their heads and gave him a nod, a fist, even a thumb-up, before turning and changing their, "No justice, no peace," into a loud, resounding, "BLACK LIVES MATTER! BLACK LIVES MATTER!"

Toya focused her camera on the young woman with the sign. Her voice strained, and a thick vein in her neck pulsed as she yelled. Toya caught her as she raised her sign higher in the air, screaming "BLACK LIVES" as she pushed it up, screaming "MATTER" when she brought it down. She turned to face Toya then, and yelled directly into the camera. She switched her sign around. The back side read STRANGE FRUIT, each letter carefully written in even, thick black letters with a series of green and red Frooties wrappers stapled along the bottom. She stopped chanting and stared at Toya through the camera, as if she could look right through the lens and into her eyes. She squared her jaw and held the sign steady. Letting the two words, which were really a whole sentence, an entire story, a lesson in history, really sink in. Toya swallowed. She snapped another picture.

"Strange fruit," Toya said. She took one more shot then lowered her camera.

"Were you filming?" the woman asked.

"No," Toya said. "Should I have been?"

"If you want to get the sounds of our voices! If you want footage of the momentum that's building! The whole energy of right here! Right now!" She pointed at the ground, her chest heaving and voice straining with excitement.

Toya chuckled and sighed.

"I say something funny?" The woman put her sign down, sticking the wooden handle into the grass.

"No," Toya said. "You sound like a friend of mine. The energy can be captured in a photograph, you know." She held the camera out from her neck to review some of the shots. "Come here. Check this one out."

Toya tilted her camera and the woman came closer. She smelled like eucalyptus and shea butter. She leaned into Toya, putting her hand on Toya's arm to angle the screen away from the sun. The touch, as slight as it was, felt electric. This woman was electric. Toya cleared her throat, and the woman glanced up at her with a sly smile before turning her attention to the monitor.

"Wow," she whispered.

The shot caught the children, the toddlers surrounding the woman with gray dreads, jumping up to chant with raised fists. The tiny ponytails of the girls, their barrettes yanking the ends of their braids up, frozen in mid-air, the ashy elbows of the boys bent for the fist pump, and the colorful shirts and shoelaces of them all flying up with the effort. Their faces lit up with excitement, their mouths forming the words, tongues against teeth, as, without even knowing it, they yelled for their lives.

Toya flipped to another shot. One of the woman herself. The cut of her triceps and lines of veins in her wrists and forearms as she lifted her sign. The sunlight kissing the sheen of sweat glowing against her skin, and her neck, elegant, almost majestic as she stretched taller, made herself bigger and louder than ever before. Toya had caught her mid-chant as well, her profile crisp and in focus against the intentionally blurred backdrop of the crowd, the trees, the clouds. She turned to another one. A close-up of the sign. Just the woman's hands around the wooden base, the words black and intentional, pulsing almost, supernatural.

"Strange fruit," Toya said.

"Yeah," she whispered, mesmerized by the photograph of herself. "Billie Holiday."

"Clever." Toya moved the camera and set it back against her chest.

She picked up her sign. "It ain't about being clever. It's about this." She raised her hand and placed it between her breasts. She gripped her shirt as if trying to find her heart to rip it out of her chest, to hand a piece of it to everyone in the park. "This young brother. J'Quan Miles. And others. So many others. I mean, this whole thing is about lynching. A modern day lynching, you know what I'm saying?" She shook her head and sighed. She looked on the verge of tears.

"I get it. I do."

"I know you do," she said. "You're here ain't you? And your pictures. You see it. You feel it. I can tell." She smiled. "You've got a great eye. A really, really great eye."

Toya looked down at her camera. She glanced back at the woman, but she had already turned, raising her sign.

"BLACK LIVES MATTER!" she yelled. More voices had joined in, the rallying cry swelling in the heat.

Folami walked up, and Toya jumped.

"Hey," she said. "I was looking for you. You want to get closer?"

"Yeah," Toya said. She snapped a few more photos of the woman and her sign. "Hey, Billie Holiday," she called. The woman turned with a smirk, raising her fist for one more shot. Toya took the picture, dropped her camera against her chest, and raised her fist to return the salute.

"You know her?" Folami asked, craning her neck over her shoulder to look at the woman.

"Not really," Toya said. "Come on." She took one last look at the woman before finally facing front to navigate through the crowd.

Toya and Folami walked around the concentrated middle of the audience, sidestepping people's blankets and plastic chairs, sliding and squeezing between groups of people standing, sitting, and leaning on trees. They got as close to the stage as they could. Toya spotted Fishbone and Kanaan, then searched the stage for Director Abasi. He sat, wide and solid as a linebacker, in a white tunic and khaki pants, a white single-weave kufi on his bald head. Next to him, Minister Abdullah from the Nation of Islam folded his arms across his chest and looked on as Reverend Jimmy Jones whispered to J'Quan Miles's parents, Juma and Yvonne Miles.

Slowly, the parents made their way to the podium. Mr. Miles stepped to the microphone and cleared his throat. He put his arm around Mrs. Miles, and she collapsed into him, covering her face with the crumpled and twisted tissues that had long lost their usefulness. He leaned forward.

"Thank you. Thank you for coming. Thank you for—" His voice cracked and he bit his lip. Mr. Miles dropped his head in grief. The couple folded into each other in grief. Their sobs choking everyone, breaking every heart in the park. Mrs. Miles straightened herself and looked out at everyone. She wiped her face with the rolled and knotted tissue then balled it into her fist.

Mrs. Miles leaned toward the microphone. "We thank you all for coming. For caring about J'Quan and for caring about... about us," she said. The breeze nearly swallowed her slight, trembling voice. "Us being here together will send a message about our son's...our son's..."

"MURDER!" someone yelled out from the crowd. The park exploded in cheers and screams, raised fists and nodding heads.

"BLACK LIVES MATTER! BLACK LIVES MATTER!" erupted from the crowd. Booming voices yelling "NO JUSTICE, NO PEACE!" and "JUSTICE FOR J'QUAN, JAIL TIME FOR VAUGHN!" made their way into the cacophony of chants and cheers complemented by clapping hands and bobbing signs.

"Well," Mr. Miles said. He cleared his throat then looked down at his wife and found his voice. "Well, we just hope that by y'all being here today, that everyone who is here and even those who ain't but that care about our...our situation...will help justice get served. All we want is justice for our son." The couple looked out at the crowd then at Reverend Jimmy Jones who was already making his way back to the podium, wiping his brow with a checkered handkerchief.

"Thank you," The couple said together. "JUSTICE FOR J'QUAN!" they yelled into the microphone in unison. Their voices strong together where alone they trembled. They walked away from the podium, and everyone cheered, yelling "God Bless You!" "We Love You!" and "Justice for J'Quan!"

Reverend Jimmy Jones announced the information for donating to the family then introduced a choir, who instead of being on stage actually stood on the grass in front of the stage. Two rows of men and women in bright blue T-shirts, Evergreen Community in Christ Baptist Church in white lettering across the front, stood up and began swaying and clapping. A woman hummed an aching prelude to "Rough Side of the Mountain." A drummer and guitarist joined the singer, and the audience started to clap along with the bass.

Toya watched the choir. Several of the members sang through tears, dabbing their eyes with the backs of their hands. She wondered if they were thinking about J'Quan and his parents, or more than that. Or less than that. She wondered if the song, like most gospel songs, churned up all the sadness and disappointment and exhaustion of their lives, their history. She wondered if Kanaan was right. Were they weak for never fighting back, for always just holding hands and humming and singing and waiting and asking for justice? Toya looked around at the crowd then back at the choir. The song reached its climax and everyone was getting into it. The song was about waiting. About praying and swaying over some vague disappointment or sadness then waiting for something to happen, waiting for a miracle. She wanted something more. A song that called this exactly what it was, a song that exposed very specifically what was happening in the community, how horrible, how clearly horrible it was. They should have sung "Strange Fruit."

CHAPTER TWELVE

Director Abasi took the podium. He looked out at the audience, a look of pride dueling with a twitching expression of expectation. He leaned forward to the microphone. "BLOOD!" he said. "BLOOD!" He stepped back and dropped his head, his chin touching his chest. The brilliant white of his kufi and tunic seemed to glow against his blue-black skin.

Toya, who had moved to get closer to the stage in order to film Dr. Abasi's speech, raised her camera to catch his stance. The way he stood, head bowed, arms flexing as he gripped the sides of the podium. He rocked, reeling off the sound of his own voice. She snapped a shot, then another. When he lifted his head, he looked pained. Toya took one last picture, capturing the strain in his eyes, the wrinkles in his forehead and around his frowning mouth, the shadows beneath his eyes and flare of his nostrils, before setting up the tripod.

Toya set the camera to record then stepped back from it. She nodded at Folami, who looked back at her with a small smile.

"This is going to be good," Folami said. "You sure you don't want to get closer?" She gestured to a spot nearer the stage where Kanaan, Fishbone, and a small group of men in a random collection of suits and dashikis stood waiting.

"Nah," Toya said. "This is good. I want to be able to get a few wide shots of everyone on the stage." She peered into the viewfinder. "You can get closer if you want."

"You sure?"

"Yeah. Go ahead." Toya smiled. She watched Folami make her way over to Kanaan and Fishbone. The three of them looked over at her, and she raised her fist in their direction.

Director Abasi spoke softly into the microphone. "Blood." He flexed his biceps as he gripped the podium, the bulk of him, solid muscles forged through clean eating and daily fitness, seemed to swell as he surveyed the crowd. A thoughtful, direct man, he always knew how to reach who he needed to reach, how to say what he needed to say. Nothing and no one stopped his message. Though he spent much of the seventies in jail, his letters to his son and the community at large sparked fires in the bellies of activists and organizers across the world. The letters were collected and published, *Liberation: An Urgency*, and even the love letters to his then-wife made political science and Africana Studies reading lists nationwide.

"We are bathed in it. We are drowning in it. Blood. Our blood," Director Abasi said.

Toya looked around. All eyes on Director Abasi and not a single person moving. She turned her attention back to the stage where J'Quan's parents sat holding each other, Mrs. Miles's head resting on her husband's chest, her arms wrapped around his waist. The only person not looking at Director Abasi, she stared at the floor of the stage, unblinking. She looked up and seemed to stare into Toya's eyes. Toya looked away.

The audience, transfixed, seemed to lean forward collectively, everyone getting closer and closer to the stage. Director Abasi took a deep breath before continuing.

"Now, I don't know about you, but I remember the bloodshed of our brothers on the front line of the movement in the fifties and sixties. We were fighting then, standing up to the system, prepared to meet the snapping teeth of police dogs, the burning mist of tear gas, and the bone-cracking blows of batons." He stopped. He closed his eyes as if going back in time. His jaw tightened then relaxed. He opened his eyes. "I was about to say something about how J'Quan Miles was different. I was about to say something about how he wasn't no activist, wasn't no freedom fighter. I was going to say that J'Quan Miles was just a young brother, minding his business, trying to get home."

Director Abasi glanced over at J'Quan's parents and nodded. He turned back to the microphone, staring out at the audience. "But that wouldn't be true. J'Quan Miles WAS an activist. He WAS a freedom fighter. He was these things because he was an Afrikan man. As an Afrikan man, his blood, his very life, makes him a powerful thing. Since his blood made him a man, and they say a man is supposed to get life, and liberty, and prosperity, and justice, we would expect his life, his blood, to be taken more seriously. Unless of course…" Director Abasi lowered his voice, "unless they didn't see J'Quan Miles as a man. Unless of course they don't see any of us as men."

Everyone on the stage shifted in their folding chairs. Mrs. Miles lifted her head and looked over at Director Abasi, who stepped back from the podium and clenched his fists at his side.

Director Abasi dipped his head toward the mic to continue, "Now, I don't want to disrespect this space, the peace of the afternoon so to speak." He looked over his shoulders then back out at the crowd. "But I am going to ask you a question. Just one question." He cleared his throat. "If they, and I trust we all know who 'they' is—"

"PIGS!" someone yelled up toward the stage. A few people applauded.

"If they deal in blood, can only understand progress and livelihood as it relates to the spilling of blood, OUR BLOOD, how do we communicate with them? What language must we speak to make them understand that we too are men? What seems to be the only way they know how to communicate?"

"BLOOD!" the small but loud group of men yelled from the one side of the stage. Folami and Fishbone looked at each other while Kanaan lifted his fist and continued the chant.

"BLOOD! BLOOD! BLOOD!" they yelled. More voices joined the chant, the loud, determined voices of women and the high-pitched, uneven voices of children. "BLOOD! BLOOD! BLOOD!"

Toya quickly stopped the recording and detached the camera from the tripod. She glanced over at where Folami stood and debated whether she should go get her before heading to a new spot. Folami had linked arms with a big, tall woman with Nubian knots and a couple of the men in dashikis, and the group of them rocked back and forth as the chanting picked up momentum. Toya shrugged and packed up her equipment and, camera swinging on her neck, carried her bag back to the spot she stood before. Near the back, off to the side, she was better able to survey the whole of the audience for the best shots.

She lifted her camera and zoomed in on the angry, trembling lips, the clenched, pumping fists, and wet, hungry eyes. Her finger moved rapidly to capture the faces, all the faces. A woman with olive skin and hazel eyes reflecting the sunlight, her very pupils on fire, her long, straight hair held back with a band of Kente cloth, screamed with a snarl, "BLOOD!"

A man, his head lifted toward the sky, his hair an orderly and intricate system of winding cornrows, yelled up to the sun, "BLOOD!" Young children, their eyes wide with wonder and fear, looked up at shouting parents and elders, mumbled the words with uncertainty, their lips trembling and barely moving. Toya scanned the crowd for Folami, zooming in as close as she could to navigate the contorted faces and pumping fists. She wanted to capture Folami's reaction. She wanted to see her framed in the moment. Was she chanting for blood? Was she afraid or energized? Was she still rocking in a group or had she broken free to give herself over to the energy swelling up around them? Toya searched the crowd but didn't find her.

"BLOOD!" Director Abasi spoke with force into the microphone, pumping his fist, "BLOOD! BLOOD! BLOOD!"

The chanting became louder, faster, a great pounding of the word into the air. Then, a drum beat. A bass kick. A clanging of keys and the shrill crashing of symbols. Pain became song, a low humming from the choir. Toya focused on the choir as they rose from their folding chairs, trampled the grass with stomping feet to the downbeat of their clapping hands. An energy, mysterious and powerful, rose up all around Toya, and she wanted so much to capture it, to document it.

The melodic, heart-wrenching wailing of the lead singer rose up and out as she opened her arms, her bright blue T-shirt stretching across her large, heaving bosom, Evergreen Community in Christ straining between her round, rolling shoulders. She bent over at the waist, and when she stood, she brought her voice, and the voices of a million others with her, the depth of it reaching beneath the blood-stained ground, the scorched earth, the width of it reaching out to the coasts, diving down and bringing up the voices of ancestors from beneath the ocean floor.

"I HAD A MIGHTY HARD TIME" she sang out. "I HAD A MIGHTY HARD TIME!"

The choir stopped humming and looked at the lead singer. Toya watched her with the viewfinder and snapped a picture as her body folded back, all of her arching toward the sky. She couldn't stop snapping, the shutter clicking rapid-fire, catching every second as if at any moment the vocalist would ascend to heaven. Her eyes closed, she tilted her head back and wailed with the thumping bass drum, quick press of keyboard keys, and the now-whispering high hat. "I HAD A MIGHTY HARD TIME. BUT I'M ON MY WAY!"

The choir needed only a second to recognize the song. The band kept steady and the voices rose up around their rhythm. "I'm on my way. I'm on my way." The refrain simple and true. "I'm on my way." Toya panned out, a wide shot of the choir, the people on the stage. The reverend and minister, J'Quan Miles's parents, each of them reaching out to hold each other's hands.

They joined the choir, "I'm on my way. I'm on my way. I'm on my way."

Director Abasi kept his own refrain, and a few voices rose to hold steady the fierce call for blood. "Blood! Blood! Blood!" Director Abasi chanted, and deep, rumbling voices from all corners of the park made the cry for blood the baseline to the song, a remix of old and new, of faith and action, the tenors and basses from the choir, singing out, "I'm on my way" while some of the audience, Director Abasi leading the chant, called out, "Blood! Blood! Blood!"

The lead singer pushed forward with her choir family behind her. "IF YOU WON'T GO, DON'T HINDER ME! I'M ON MY WAY!"

Toya dropped her camera against her chest. Her own voice a shock to her ears as she joined in with the choir, who, catching the spirit of their leader, clapped and bounced their shoulders to the beat. "I'm on my way. I'm on my way. I'm on my way!"

"IF YOU WON'T GO, DON'T HINDER ME! I'M ON MY WAY TO CANAAN LAND! I'M ON MY WAY! GLORY HALLELUJAH! I HAD A MIGHTY HARD TIME, BUT I'M ON MY WAY! A MIGHTY HARD TIME! DON'T YOU HINDER ME! I'M ON MY WAY!" The choir leader's voice screamed out, her face contorted with the effort, a trembling hand raised up to the sky, sweat pouring down her face. The choir's clapping sped up, the drummer rapped on the snare to build momentum.

Director Abasi stepped back to the podium, and "BLOOD! BLOOD! BLOOD!" pounded from the speakers with the thump of the bass drum.

"Blood! Blood! Blood!" tumbled from Toya's lips, her hands burning as she clapped in time with the snare. Her feet pounded the grass beneath her feet in time with the bass. "I'm on my way! I'm on my way!" She sang with the choir, tears burning in the corners of her eyes. "BLOOD! BLOOD! BLOOD!" Bursting from her throat as she wiped at her eyes. Toya's throat hurt, but her voice kept singing both songs, chanting both choruses. "Blood! Blood! Blood! I'm on my way! I'm on my way!" Full on crying, Toya's tears came too fast to wipe and snot ran from her nose. She tasted the salty-sweet mixture of them both every time she opened her mouth. She swallowed and kept singing, kept yelling, her hands numb. "Blood! Blood! Blood! I'm on my way! I'm on my way!"

Everyone around Toya began to dance, wild flailing of arms and heads thrown back in passion. Feet stomping and backs bucking to the beats and the voices. Praise dances and African dances. Through her tears, Toya looked down at her hands, clapping so hard she felt it in her shoulders, her knees raising to stomp her feet into the grass and dirt. Her body lurched forward then sprang back.

Toya sang, "I'm on my way! I'm on my way! Blood! Blood! Blood!" She couldn't catch her breath. She looked around, everyone dancing and screaming and chanting. She panted, her hands still clapping, her body moving to the sound of the music and the voices. Toya blinked against the tears that kept coming. She couldn't keep still. She couldn't stop crying or clapping or dancing. It scared her. She felt energized but afraid. Afraid of the way her body moved. Afraid of what she was feeling.

Toya's camera swung as she danced, everything becoming a mix of colors and voices and drumbeats and sunlight and tears and smiles and snarls and sky and wailing and hands and lights and voices and screams and clouds and grass. Toya felt herself opening up, a clarity—every color glowing, every heartbeat echoing her own, every breath filling her chest—claimed her, and suddenly everything made sense. The movement, her heart, her power, her identity, her charge. All of it blew up inside her, screaming and demanding to be let out. Toya's face flushed, her temples throbbed, her vision blurred. Dizzy. Weak. Confused. Scared. Reaching, trying to find something to grab, to hold on to, to keep herself from falling. Nothing. There was nothing to hold to, nothing to cling to, she was all she had, all she could count on. She collapsed under the weight of the reality, the urgency of here and now bent her knees, and she bowed to its power.

In the darkness behind her eyelids, Toya saw faces and more faces, familiar and unfamiliar. She heard voices and more voices, screams and whispers. Trapped in a box, no light, no exit. Her mother's voice. Soft, timid, seeking forgiveness. Toya reached out, her hands fumbling for the wall. Nothing to hold on to, nothing to calm the swirling or stabilize the sensation of falling into oblivion. Then hands. Toya felt hands. Warm, strong, coaxing her open, wider and wider. Folami's hands. The press of her fingers, the scratch of her nails. A gripping, too tight, breaking her skin. Blood. Blood splattering on signs and pictures. Fire and smoke consuming everything around her. Buses empty and cars abandoned. The streets filling with bodies, standing and prone. Eyes searching and ears straining to hear. Flashing lights. Toya heard her own voice screaming in her ears.

Chapter Thirteen

Toya opened her eyes slowly. She looked up, disoriented and aching all over. The hard ground beneath her, and above, the soothing blue of the sky, puffs of gentle clouds. Then, a friendly face.

"Billie Holiday," Toya whispered.

"Slow. Slow and easy now," the woman said in a calm, clear voice. She wrapped a strong arm around Toya's waist and sat her up. She gripped Toya's elbow with firm fingers.

The woman smiled. "My name is Nina, actually." She helped Toya stand then and placed her hands, warm and strong and sure on her shoulders. "Are you good?" Her dark brown eyes searched; wrinkles of concern appeared between her neat eyebrows, sunlight glinting off the silver stud in her nose.

Toya nodded and cleared her throat. "Yeah." She looked around. A small group of women and children had gathered. They smiled in understanding and pressed their hands together in relief as Toya stretched her back and rolled her shoulders. She nodded a thank you in their direction as they reached around to gather their children. The park had started to clear. People walked slowly toward the edges of the park while some stood around talking and hugging. A few people still danced though the band slowly dismantled their instruments to pack up. The stage, empty except for Reverend Jones and Director Abasi, seemed farther away than it had all afternoon.

"You fainted," Nina said. She squeezed Toya's shoulders. Toya rolled them once more beneath Nina's massaging fingers.

"Yeah," Toya said. "Crazy, huh? How long was I out?" A little disoriented, Toya scanned the stage area once more, looking for Folami, even hoping to see Kanaan or Fishbone.

Nina pursed her lips. "Not long," she said. "It's no big deal. It's hot and...crowded...and...It's no big deal." She shrugged and moved her hands down Toya's arms before taking Toya's hands in her own. "You're okay now though, right? That's all that really matters."

"Yeah. I'm good. Thank you," Toya said. She gripped Nina's hands to reassure her.

"I was hoping to see you again," Nina said. She didn't release Toya's hands. A current of attraction passing between them.

"Oh yeah," Toya said. She glanced down at their joined hands then looked up at Nina. "What for?" She slowly pulled her hands away. Nina smiled at her. Toya returned the smile then blushed as Nina's hands reluctantly released her fingers.

"Just wanted to see you again," Nina said. "Tell you my real name. Get yours. Maybe see what else you shot this afternoon. I'm sure you got some amazing images."

"I did. At least, I think so. I haven't looked at them yet and when that choir started..." Toya sighed and scratched at the back of her neck nervously. Still a bit disoriented, she hadn't a clue why she fainted. When she tried to recall the moments before, she saw flashes of scenes from the rally mixed with scenes from when she was out—not sure what was real and what wasn't, everything she tried to recall came back dream-like and unclear.

"Well, let's see what you got." Nina stepped closer to Toya, who rolled her shoulders then lifted the camera and turned on the monitor.

"I took these while the director was speaking," Toya said, scrolling through a few shots of the audience rapt by Abasi's speech. She stopped on a photo of J'Quan's parents.

"Wow…" Nina said.

"Toya."

Nina looked up from the monitor. "Toya," she said with a smile.

Toya went through a few more photos before getting to the close-ups of the people chanting and the lead singer bursting into song. Sunlight set profiles aglow in amber and crimson; bodies contorted with passion and protest—clenched fists and tight jaws, arched backs and strained necks.

"Toya, I'm…I'm speechless," Nina said. She looked into Toya's eyes.

Toya looked away and cleared her throat. "I just wanted to capture the energy."

"Yo, you did that and then some."

Toya scrolled through the pictures back toward the beginning. She stopped on the last photo she snapped of Nina, right before she had gone to get video of Abasi. The picture, a quick snapshot of Nina as she looked over her shoulder, a fist raised, a small, mischievous smile playing at the corner of her shapely lips, needed a little editing but had a gritty, hurried, urgent feel to it that seemed intentional. She held out the camera for Nina to see herself, simple, beautiful, and artistic.

Nina glanced down at the monitor then leaned in closer. She placed a hand on Toya's arm and squeezed as she stared down at herself in the photo. "This is…this is…"

"You," Toya said. "This is you." She smiled.

Nina looked up at Toya. She smiled.

"TOYA!" Folami called out.

Both Toya and Nina jumped and looked over their shoulders. Folami came running over to Toya, holding a bottle of water.

Nina looked at Folami then looked at Toya. She took a step back then slid her hands into the pockets of her denim vest. The movement struck Toya as abrupt, and she raised an eyebrow in Nina's direction. Nina shrugged and smiled. Toya set her camera against her chest.

"Hey, Folami," Toya said.

"I've been looking for you! Where have you been?" Folami held out her water. "You look hot and exhausted. Drink some water."

"I'm fine, but thank you." Toya unscrewed the cap and drank the water down in loud gulps, the plastic bottle crushing against itself. The water was warm, but it was wet, and she welcomed it with each swallow.

Nina and Folami eyed each other. Nina rocked back on her heels and looked around the park. Toya brought the bottle from her lips and nudged her chin in Nina's direction.

"Folami, this is Nina," Toya said.

Nina raised a slender hand. "Hi."

Folami smiled a tight-lipped smile. "Hello," she said.

Toya drank the last of the water then recapped the empty bottle. "We were—"

"NINA! NINA! LET'S GO!" a booming voice called from a nearby tree, where a group of women and men dressed in patchwork denim skirts, ripped up jeans, and African print tunics stood packing up their chairs and signs. A tall white boy in a denim vest like Nina's waved his hand to beckon her over.

Nina shrugged and smiled at Toya. "I gotta go. But I'm glad you're okay," she said, her eyes crinkling in concern. "Thank you for showing me your pictures. They're beautiful. You're beautiful." She smiled at Toya then at Folami. She raised her fist. "All power to the people," she said before turning and jogging over to her friends.

"Thank you," Toya called after her. Nina pumped her fist in the air, but didn't turn around. Toya watched her walk away.

"Why wouldn't you be okay?" Folami asked. She knelt to zip up Toya's camera bag, stuffing the protruding leg from the tripod deeper inside before pulling the zipper closed. She picked up the bag and slung it over her shoulder.

"What?" Toya said, finally tearing her eyes away from Nina and her friends as they walked farther away.

"I said," Folami said with irritation. "Why wouldn't you be okay?"

"No reason," Toya said. She tried to reassure Folami with a quick smile. "What's the plan?"

Folami cut her eyes then shook her head. "Whatever. We're heading to the car. Director Abasi wants us back in St. Pete so we can meet at the center tomorrow morning. Early. He says we need a strong organizing strategy in case Vaughn isn't charged. Odds are he won't be. They ain't said it officially, but the director said we need to be ready and trump tight with a plan when the decision comes down."

Toya nodded. She debated whether or not to tell Folami that she fainted. She wanted to tell her, but telling her about fainting would mean telling her about what happened right before she fainted—the way the music and chanting invaded her, a possession almost. She didn't know what happened exactly, and she didn't know what to do with the visions she had, the charge she felt from her toes to the top of her head. She looked over her shoulder once more though Nina and her friends had long gone. Maybe she didn't have to say anything at all. She was all right. Perhaps that was all that mattered.

Chapter Fourteen

The Impala crept through the blaring tail and headlights on McCarthy Avenue and finally made it to I-75 South. Merging into the lighter than expected traffic, it seemed that just a few people must have made the drive from down state to Evergreen. Folami said most of the people she met had been from Atlanta, Valdosta, Gainesville, and Tallahassee. Fishbone mentioned that he had met a few people from New York and a couple from Memphis, but other than that, everyone he met lived in Evergreen or Tallahassee. Kanaan, like Toya, was silent. They drove that way for a good while, Folami and Fishbone recounting people they had met and organizations they noticed in attendance. They shared a laugh at the expense of the white people handing out their peace bracelets. She elbowed Toya when Fishbone said, "You know we can't have nothing." Toya forced a smile and returned her attention to the passing cars and farmland blanketed in darkness.

"I'm excited to see what our next move is going to be," Folami said. "I have some ideas. I definitely think we should incorporate music. Did you feel the energy once the choir and the band turned up?"

At the mention of the choir and the band, Toya stared more intensely out the window. The darkness of the sky and blur of trees made it easy to ignore the uneasiness that churned in her belly. She pressed her head against the window to look up at the stars.

"That was fire," Fishbone said. "I felt that shit in my chest."

"What about you, Toya?" Folami asked. "Didn't you feel the energy in the rally go from ten to one thousand when the—"

"The music is beside the point," Kanaan said. He had only removed his sunglasses when they got to the car and slid behind the wheel to drive. "It hyped up the mood, but that shit was a distraction. Did you hear what Director Abasi was saying? Now that is what got me turned up. That's what got me hype." Kanaan sped up and dipped over into the left lane to pass a car. He moved back over to the right lane and settled back in his seat, cruising.

Toya stared out the window. The traffic thinned more and more as they got closer to Tampa, and with only sixty more miles to I-275, she looked forward to getting home. She didn't want to talk about her experience with all the others in the car. She needed to talk to Folami alone, wanted to ask her once and for all what she wanted to do. The way the music moved her and the excitement of meeting someone new made Toya realize that she was ready to strike out on her own, that she had energy and ideas that were being stifled. She wanted Folami to be part of this renewal, but was also prepared to leave her and RiseUP! behind if the plans demanded it.

"Of course," Folami said. "The director is a powerful speaker. We know that. I do think he was a little harsh though. All the blood talk seemed kind of morbid. Mr. and Mrs. Miles didn't look pleased at all."

Kanaan chuckled. "Morbid?"

"Fuck morbid," Kanaan said. "This struggle is about life and death. Ain't no way to talk about it without talking about blood. About death."

Folami sighed and sat back. Fishbone looked out the window. Kanaan seemed to take the hint that no one was interested in another lecture like the one he'd treated them to on the way to the rally. He exhaled loudly and sat up to maneuver around another slow moving car.

Two quick whoops from a police siren woke Toya up. She hadn't realized she'd nodded out. She sat up, Folami and Fishbone following suit; apparently, all three of them had dozed off. The red and blue flashing lights lit into the car.

"What did you do?" Fishbone whispered.

Kanaan looked over at him then rolled his eyes and shook his head. He pressed the button to roll down his window then he rested both hands on the steering wheel and looked straight ahead.

The car felt like a gas chamber right before they flipped the switch, a sense of impending doom making the space tight and full and nauseous. No one moved.

The officer finally climbed out of the car and walked slowly up to the Impala. He peered into the backseat, his mirrored glasses hanging from the middle of his shirt. He squinted and frowned at Toya and Folami. He walked up to the driver's side window and placed his hand on top of his holster.

"License, registration, and proof of insurance." His said, his southern accent near nonexistent with the exception of a slight twang that held on like barnacles to the ends of his words.

Kanaan took a deep breath and looked over at Fishbone. Fishbone held up his hands to show the officer they were empty, then he moved slowly and carefully, reaching forward to unlatch the glove compartment. He guided the door onto his lap so it wouldn't snap and paused for the officer, who as if on cue, tilted his head to peer inside. Fishbone showed his hands once more and used one hand to take out the clear envelope that held the vehicle registration and insurance cards. He carefully handed it to Kanaan, who lifted his hands from the steering wheel, fingers spread, and held up in surrender. He took the envelope from Fishbone and held it out to the officer.

The officer stared at the envelope. His thick mustache twitching under his pinched nose, his jaws working as if he was chewing the world's smallest piece of gum. "I'm supposed to read it through the envelope?" he said. His fingers drummed his holster.

Kanaan pulled the envelope back slowly and held it awkwardly against the steering wheel as he worked the papers out with his fingers. He held the registration and insurance cards out to the officer. His hand shook. He noticed it the same time Toya did and tried to stop it, but to no avail. The officer snatched the papers.

"Why you moving so slow? Don't you want to get out of here?" The officer sighed and thumbed through the registration and insurance cards. He leaned forward and looked through the window at all of them. He licked the inside of his mouth with his tongue as if he were cleaning his teeth with his own spit. He held the papers. "This is just registration and insurance."

Kanaan took a deep breath. He lifted himself up from the seat and pulled his wallet out of his back pocket. He slid his license from the plastic window inside his wallet and handed it to the officer.

"Kevin Reynolds," the officer said. He stared at Kanaan and narrowed his eyes. He looked back at the registration.

Folami and Toya exchanged confused looks. Folami shrugged. The officer tilted his head to look in the backseat. Folami sat up straight and stared straight ahead.

"Who is…" The officer stopped and stared down at the registration. He sighed. "Who is Chuh-muh Ah-beezy?"

"Chuma Abasi," Kanaan said. "He owns the car, sir. There's a notarized letter in the envelope describing the organizational use of the car. It's the community car for Rise—"

"I don't give a shit," the officer said, cutting Kanaan off. "A notarized letter." The officer chuckled and shook his head. He went back to Kanaan's license. "You know your license is expired?"

"No, I did not realize that, sir," Kanaan said.

"It's been expired for months," he said.

"I did not realize that, sir," Kanaan repeated. His hands rested on the steering wheel, his gaze set straight ahead.

"Look at me when I'm talking to you," the officer said.

Kanaan faced the officer.

"Don't you think keeping your license up to date is important?"

"Yes, sir." Kanaan nodded.

"I can't tell," the officer said. "You also don't think it's important to signal when you change lanes. Seem to me you don't think any of these little rules and regulations are important. Is that right? You think it's important to follow rules and regulations?"

"No, sir."

"No?" He leaned forward, holding the papers and Kanaan's license in one hand and resting the other on his holster again. "You probably make up your own rules, don't you?"

"Yes, sir. I mean, no, sir, that ain't right. No, sir I…" Kanaan bit his lip and took a deep breath. He shook his head. "No, sir, I don't make up my own rules. I just…" He sighed, frustration mounting his voice.

"You nervous, boy?" the officer said. "You got any reason to be nervous?"

Kanaan's shoulders tensed and he dropped his head. It was probably all he could do to keep from unraveling. As much as Kanaan irritated Toya, she wanted to reach up around the headrest and place her hands on his shoulders. She wanted to comfort him. She slid her hands under her thighs to fight the urge.

Kanaan slowly lifted his head. "No, sir. I am not nervous."

The officer smacked his tongue against his teeth. "Let's see what we got here. Sit tight."

They all sat motionless, staring straight ahead as the officer went back to his car. After a few seconds, they all exhaled but didn't speak. Fishbone slouched in his seat, nervously rolling one of his dreads between his fingers. Folami sat straight up, her shoulders hunched and jaws clenched. She bounced her leg and bit at her bottom lip. Toya swallowed and leaned forward to whisper at Kanaan.

"Is there anything else we need to know?" Toya said.

Kanaan jerked his head up and looked over his shoulder at Toya and Folami in the back before facing straight ahead.

"Well?" Toya sat up. Kanaan's name and expired license aside, she couldn't help but recall the visitors to the center before they left for the rally.

"Just be cool. He can't search the car without a warrant," Kanaan said.

Folami's head snapped toward Kanaan. "What? Why would he search the car? What would he find? What's in the car, Kanaan? What have you gotten us into? Oh shit. Oh shit," Folami's voice rose in pitch. "Oh shit. Oh shit."

"I said RELAX!" Kanaan yelled. He looked over his shoulder. They all turned around to look out the back window. "Face front!" Kanaan said. "You're making us look suspicious."

Fishbone sunk down lower in his seat. A dread in his mouth. He chewed it and sank even lower, his knees crammed underneath the glove compartment. Folami, breathing hard but quiet, stared straight ahead. Toya looked at her and Fishbone. She leaned forward against the driver seat.

"What the fuck do you have in this car?" Toya said through clenched teeth.

A bright beam of fluorescent white light blasted into the car, and they all froze. The intrusive light became a spotlight on their argument, making everything hard and raw. The fine hairs on their faces, the trembles in their chins, all visible.

"What do you have in the car, Kanaan?" Folami said in a soft whisper. "You got us driving around down here, at night, and you know how the cops are down here. And with the J'Quan Miles rally and the news and—"

"Would you just shut the fuck up?" Kanaan said.

"Hey," Toya said. "Don't talk to her like that."

Kanaan twisted around in his seat. "Look, I'm the one whose ass is on the line right now. Mine. So unless you got a way to keep me from getting hauled off right the fuck now, you both can shut the fuck up."

"Come on, y'all," Fishbone said. "Calm down. Maybe he'll—"

"Maybe he'll what, Fish?" Kanaan said. He shook his head and shrugged. "Let us go? Yeah, right. Is you fucking stupid?"

"Kanaan!" Toya said.

"What!?"

Kanaan and Toya stared at each other. She knew what was wrong. The way he fidgeted, spun around this way and that, his head on a swivel. He was afraid. They all were. The light burned on, reminding them that they were being watched. Folami rocked gently and stared out the windshield. Fishbone chewed at his dreads. A shadow danced in front of the light. Kanaan faced forward, his hands on the steering wheel.

The officer walked back to the car. Toya sat back just as he reached her window. He tapped the glass with his pen and chuckled when she jumped.

He stood at the driver's side window. "Look like all y'all a bit jumpy this evening." He chewed at his tiny piece of gum then spit off to the side. "Where you coming from?" he said. He knew where they were coming from. He had to know.

"The rally," Toya said. Folami looked at her, surprised and obviously afraid. The police officer turned his head and reared back in disbelief.

"I wasn't talking to you," he said. "Don't you know how to keep your women quiet?" he said. "You look like a strong, take-charge kinda fella. Would seem to me that you could keep yo' bitches in check," he said to Kanaan, though he stared at Toya and Folami.

Toya clenched her fists at her side, her nails digging into her palms with so much force she nearly broke the skin. Toya looked at the officer and bit at the inside of her jaw to keep quiet. Without knowing what Kanaan had in the car, there was no way to talk to this officer, no way to defend themselves or demand respect, no way to control the events if the officer felt threatened or provoked, even as his behavior threatened and provoked them.

The officer shook his head. He looked down at Kanaan. His face wide and pale, except for two rosy blotches at his cheekbones. His pulled his thin, dry lips against his crooked teeth and wiggled his mustache as he looked down at the papers and license he held in his hand.

"The rally, huh?" he said, rocking back on his heels and catching himself as he pitched himself forward slightly. "You know driving with an expired license is a crime?"

"Yes, sir," Kanaan said. He looked at the officer and nodded. His hands rested on the steering wheel at ten and two. His hands rested gently as if he were afraid to grip, as if any movement of muscles in his hands or wrists, any movement of his fingers would be considered a threat.

"You gotta license?" the officer said to Fishbone, who let his dread drop from his lips but didn't look in the officer's direction.

Fishbone shook his head.

"Your mouth don't work?" the officer said. "You got a gash in the back speaking out of turn and a waste-of-space wing man afraid to answer questions? You need to upgrade your crew, boy." He sighed and looked at Fishbone and Kanaan in disgust. He turned his head and leaned into the window to stare into the backseat.

"What about y'all? Either of y'all got a license?"

Folami nodded. Toya crossed her arms and bit at the inside of her jaw. She didn't trust her body or her voice. The officer stared at her. She stared back.

"You hard of hearing?" he said, staring Toya down.

"No," she said.

The officer looked at her expectantly. He smirked when he realized that Toya wasn't going to call him "sir."

"Well?" he said.

"Yes. I have a license." Toya didn't look at him. She looked at the back of the driver's seat. She stared at the soft gray upholstery. If she looked at the officer, her eyes would betray her, would contradict the calm with which she spoke.

The officer pointed at Toya. "Get up here and drive then."

Everyone in the car exhaled and slouched a little when he said it. He chuckled and stood back. He handed Kanaan his license and the car registration then stood up straight.

"Y'all don't know how easy I'm taking it on y'all tonight. I know what rally y'all coming from, and I really don't give a shit. But I know how you people are. Pulling the race card and ready to call the newspapers and ask for lawyers and reverends like you aren't responsible for your own actions." He shook his head. "I'm going back to my car," he said. He pointed at Toya, "You've got thirty seconds to get your black ass up here behind this steering wheel"—he pointed at Kanaan—"and you've got that same thirty seconds to get your black ass in this backseat. Then I want all four of your protesting black asses out of my county. I make myself clear?"

They all nodded. He shook his head once more and walked back to his car. Kanaan and Toya made the switch in quick, nervous silence. Settled behind the steering wheel, Toya adjusted the rearview mirror, put on her signal, and pulled onto the empty, dark highway. The tense quiet of the car pressed at her temples and she could barely concentrate. Toya watched the shimmering white highway lines lead them into the darkness. The sheriff followed them for a few miles then turned off at an opening between the cement highway partition, the blue and silver "Sumner County" in capital letters reflecting the moonlight.

CHAPTER FIFTEEN

Toya, Fishbone, Folami, and Kanaan arrived at Fishbone's grandmother's house in South St. Pete around midnight. Toya made a U-turn at the end of the cul-de-sac and pulled in front of the ranch-style house only blocks away from Lake Maggiore. She put the car in "park" but didn't kill the engine. Thelonious Monk's fluttering keys accompanied by the soft boom-tick of drums and short blasts of trumpets filled the car; they'd driven home to the comforting sounds of public radio's late night jazz. The block was quiet and empty. Fishbone whispered a quick thanks and climbed out of the car. He walked up to the side door, keys in hand, and waited. Toya waited to see what Kanaan was going to do. She knew he stayed with Fishbone when he'd worn out his welcome at either of his baby mamas' houses.

"Am I taking you somewhere?" Toya asked.

"Nah," he said. "Here's good." He grabbed at the door handle.

"You want to get whatever the hell you have in the trunk?" Toya said, not a drop of patience in her voice.

"Ain't nothing in the trunk." He sighed and rolled his eyes. He cleared his throat. "It's under the seat."

Toya turned to face him. He looked away. She shook her head and faced front, getting her bearings and preparing herself for what she'd find when she reached beneath the driver's seat.

She leaned forward against the steering wheel and reached underneath the seat. Her fingers stretched and wiggled until she felt it. Cold. Steel. Toya pushed her hand farther and wrapped her fingers around the barrel. She pulled the gun slowly, wrapping her fingers around it carefully. Finally, she held the weight of it in her hand. She sat up and held the gun in her palm. Folami sat forward and gasped. She looked at Kanaan. Tears filled her eyes and her bottom lip trembled. She turned away from him, staring out the window.

Toya handed Kanaan the .45, the weight of it, coupled with the immense weight of the trouble they narrowly avoided, made her hand shake as she passed the gun toward the back of the car. Kanaan took it and began to speak.

"Just get the fuck out," Toya said.

Kanaan turned to Folami. "Look, I'm sorry—"

"Just get the fuck out of the car, Kanaan," Toya said.

He sighed and climbed out of the car. He stuffed the gun in the front of his pants and held it in place as he jogged up to the side entrance. Fishbone raised his fist in the direction of the car then pushed open the door. Kanaan followed him inside.

Toya put the car in gear and drove off. She turned the music down and drove slowly, cruising up MLK Jr. Drive, heading north. When she reached Twenty-Second Avenue South, she flipped the turn signal and moved into the left turn lane.

"Can we go to your place?" Folami said.

Toya looked at Folami over her shoulder. She didn't move. She kept staring out the window.

"Yeah," Toya said. "Whatever you want." When the light changed green, she pulled off, getting back into the main lane for MLK, and continued north. She took MLK through the curve until it became Ninth Street. She turned the music back up. Randy Crawford's silky voice encouraged by Joe Sample on keyboard crept into the backseat, and Folami finally relaxed. She looked at Toya. Toya glanced back at her and tried to smile. She tried, too.

❖

Toya parked in the small parking lot on the side of her building. They walked up the dark outdoor stairwell and up to her apartment. They both looked over the railing at the small group of men huddled in the courtyard. The men passed a blunt around between them, and only one of them looked up as Toya and Folami made their way to Toya's door.

Once inside Toya's apartment, Folami took a seat on the couch. Toya turned on the light over the stove and sat on a stool at the small breakfast bar that separated the kitchen from the living room. She realized, watching Folami sit down so easily, that she had never been to her tiny, one-bedroom apartment before. From where Folami sat, on the low, red and brown tweed sofa she'd found at a thrift store, she could see everything there was to see.

Toya didn't own a television, but just below the large square window sat two wide bookshelves filled with books, magazines, and albums. A short table in the far corner held her record player and receiver, the speakers on the floor on either side. A floor lamp and corn plant flanked the framed, blown-up photo of Fannie Lou Hamer leaning at the podium, sick and tired of being sick and tired. Just past where Toya sat, a short hallway led to the bathroom and her bedroom. She shifted on the stool.

"Were you afraid?" Folami asked.

Toya nodded, then realized that Folami wasn't looking at her, that she had hardly looked at her since she held the gun in her hand, since their failed smiles in the car. Still anxious, still scared, Folami held herself, her arms wrapped around herself and shoulders hunched forward like she had a chill in her bones she couldn't shake. The warmth of the shadowy apartment heightened the stress and insecurity that made Folami appear closed off and far away.

Toya pushed herself up from the stool and walked slowly over to Folami. She knelt in front of her and rested her hands on Folami's thighs. Folami trembled, tears streaming down her cheeks.

"Look at me," Toya said.

Folami bit her lip and blinked out more tears. She lifted her face slowly.

"You're safe here," Toya said. "I won't let anything happen to you. Ever. I won't ever let anything happen to you." The sentiment tumbled out of her mouth before she could catch it and make it less dramatic.

Folami smiled, a strained, pitiful smile, but a smile all the same. She took a deep breath and leaned forward. She pressed her lips against Toya's lips gently but with intention. Toya kissed her back with the same focused tenderness. The kiss was a comfort, a hiding, a safety. Toya hoped Folami felt it too, because with their lips pressed against each other's, their breath the same, their heartbeats the same, they hid together, and no one could touch them.

Folami pulled away. "I'm sorry," she said. She shook her head and frowned. "I didn't mean to do that."

"It's okay," Toya said.

"It's not," Folami said. She took a deep breath. "It's not okay." She slid Toya's hands off her and moved to stand. "We have boundaries now. We need them."

Toya nodded. "You're right." She moved aside to let Folami pass. Toya was too exhausted to go into how she felt. She wanted to tell Folami that she hadn't meant what she said. Not exactly. She did want her. She'd wanted her the moment she'd met her and every day since then. What she didn't want were the lies, the sneaking around, the suppression of what was obviously so strong, so right. She remembered the moment at the rally. A shifting had taken place, an opening of something once closed. She wanted to share that with Folami, so that maybe, Folami could open herself up, too.

Folami stood at the edge of the sofa and glanced down the dark hall to Toya's bedroom.

"Go ahead," Toya said. Her heart swelled against her chest, near bursting with things she wanted to say and do. "Take my bed. I'll sleep out here."

"Are you sure?"

Toya nodded.

"Thank you, Toya," Folami said. She turned and made her way to the bedroom.

Toya pushed herself up from the floor and took off her shoes. Fully clothed, she stretched out on the couch and stared at the ceiling. She looked over at her Fannie Lou Hamer poster and pushed her thoughts past Folami, through Kanaan and the gun, the officer and the director's speech. She thought of Billie Holiday, Nina, and hummed "Strange Fruit" under her breath. Toya thought about the sights and sounds of the day, the snapshots, the faces, and the music, the constant hum in her chest since the choir and chanting. She closed her eyes then opened them.

Toya sat up and reached for her phone, which sat face down on the table. She picked it up slowly. She took deep breaths in an effort to calm herself, to manage the wild beating of her heart as she accessed her voicemail. She put the phone to her ear. The beginning of the message was fuzzy silence, then breath, quick, nervous breath.

Then, her mother's voice. The sound of it, cracking and uncertain, older than Toya remembered, brought tears to her eyes. Toya listened as her mother explained that she and her father were getting a divorce. The message sounded antiseptic. Cold almost. Her mother spoke carefully, delivering the details of the impending court date as if trying not to upset Toya, as if not to disturb her father with too much emotion, as if trying to be diplomatic, still. The tone almost made Toya gag. She stopped the message before her mother finished. She placed the phone on the table and lay back down. Tears rolled from the corner of her eyes and into her ears.

"Toya," Folami whispered.

Toya opened her eyes and quickly wiped at the side of her face. Folami stood at the end of the sofa, her hands nervously pulling at the bottom of her tank top.

"What's wrong?" Toya asked, sitting up.

"Could you…" She stopped and looked down at her hands. Nervous. She was nervous. Toya had never seen Folami so nervous, didn't think she could ever be nervous. She also hadn't seen Folami afraid before, didn't think she could ever be afraid. Against her best interest, she loved her even more in the last few hours than she had before.

Folami cleared her throat, but her voice was still a whisper when she said, "Could you come lay with me?"

"Yes," Toya said without hesitation.

Toya swung her legs over the side of the sofa and stood up. Folami walked back through the short, dark hallway with Toya following close behind.

They stepped fully into the room. The streetlights poured through the open blinds, striping their bodies with soft glowing orange and fuzzy black shadows. Folami crawled into bed, sliding beneath the sheets, scooting toward the wall, leaving room for Toya, who climbed into bed next to her. Folami turned onto her side and faced the wall, her back to Toya. She settled herself against the pillow and pulled the sheet and thin blanket over her shoulder.

"Good night," Toya said, positioning herself on her back, one hand across her stomach, the other behind her head.

"Will you hold me?" Folami said into the darkness.

Toya didn't answer. Holding her would be too much, everything already teetering on the edge. Toya didn't want to fall. She had too much to figure out. Too much to balance.

Folami repeated herself. "Will you hold me?"

Toya licked her lips and started to speak, but couldn't find her voice. She couldn't say no. Didn't want to say it anyway. Peering over the edge, the beauty that lay at her feet, a belief, naive or not, that she could have it all. Toya closed her eyes and leapt. She turned on her side and wrapped her arm around Folami. Folami gripped Toya's hand and pulled her closer, pressing her ass against Toya's thighs and resting Toya's hand between her breasts. Through the thin cotton of Folami's tank top, Toya felt Folami's heart pounding, beating hard and wild against her palm. She knew the rhythm. It matched hers. It was the quick, thumping beat of being stretched too tight, a drumhead on the brink of snapping, the heartbeat of someone caught, trapped, wanting to do something, but being afraid, scared, frightened to say what you want, what you think, what you believe. The heartbeat of someone too terrified to act, too terrified to move. Just like they were a few hours before, sitting in the car, afraid, scared, terrified. Toya closed her eyes and pressed her face against the nape of Folami's neck, finally releasing the tears she'd held back all day.

❖

Toya woke up to hands. Slow moving hands. Exploring hands. Folami's slow moving, exploring hands. Her hands slid up Toya's stomach, her fingers reaching up under Toya's T-shirt, grazing the bottom of her bra. Toya opened her eyes. Folami had propped herself up on her elbow, her breathing slow and even, the sheet and blanket at her waist. She looked up at Toya and bit her bottom lip before advancing her hand, resting her palm on the cup of Toya's breast. She leaned in and kissed her. Toya kissed her back. Folami squeezed Toya's breast, gently, massaging her through her bra.

Folami kissed Toya's neck and moved her body closer, closer, closer. She lifted her leg to straddle Toya, but Toya used a hand to catch her knee.

Toya took a deep breath. "What are you doing?"

Folami blinked and sighed. With her hand still resting on Toya's breast, she smiled a tiny, introspective smile. Whatever thought she had, Toya wanted it.

"What? Tell me," Toya said.

"Toya," she said. "I don't know exactly what this is between us, but it's something." She shook her head and sighed. "Do you remember when we met?"

Toya sat up. She pulled her T-shirt down and leaned against the headboard. "Of course I remember," she said.

"You were so sweet. Even a little shy, which is funny now because you're so not." Folami chuckled.

"I remember you told me I smelled like home," Toya said.

"And you blushed," Folami said.

They looked at each other with a smile before a silence formed and hovered above their heads, an anvil of things unsaid.

"When you said you didn't want me the other night," Folami said, "it hurt." She sighed. "It made me—"

"Folami, I didn't mean—"

"Stop," Folami said. She put a hand to Toya's lips. "Let me finish. Hearing you say it. Watching you leave. It made me think about just how heavy all this shit is."

"All what shit?"

"Everything. It made me…" Folami sighed again. She shook her head.

"Made you what?" Toya said. The conversation was losing momentum, the anvil teetering, the rope giving. "Tell me. Your feelings are important. They're so important. I can't be the only one feeling things around here. I can't be."

Folami glanced up at Toya. "You aren't. I feel it. This thing between us." A tiny curl claimed the corner of her mouth. "I can't deny it. And I've been denying so much for so long. That's what I'm tired of, that's what exhausts me." She moved her fingers, light and seductive, up Toya's arm. She scooted closer. Her lips parted; her eyes told Toya stories of first kisses and first loves, promises and heartbreaks.

"I need this," Folami said. "I need you."

"I don't know what you're saying. I don't know what you want from me," Toya said.

"I want you," Folami said. "I know that now. I want you."

Folami kissed Toya. Her lips full and determined, encouraging and dismantling all at once. Toya kissed her back, and Folami's hands slid down the front of her T-shirt to the top of her jeans. Her fingers dove underneath the bottom of Toya's shirt, her warm, soft hands like silk against her belly. Folami's tongue in Toya's mouth like a cue, they undressed each other frantically then slowed way, way down.

Folami kissed Toya's forehead, the tip of her nose, her lips and chin. She rubbed her thighs against Toya, and every muscle between them clenched and released in rhythm. She kissed Toya's neck and bit her shoulder as Toya opened her legs wider. Folami opened her legs too, and turned her body slightly so that they found each other. She was hot and throbbing just like Toya; wet and slippery just like Toya. They moved together, grinding and rolling and riding each other in perfect synch. Their coming together a surprise, the clench and growl, the shaking. Toya wrapped her arms around Folami, pulled her close, and flipped her over. They greeted the dawn, an urgency of hands and lips, a sharing of sighs and chorus of soft moans.

❖

Toya woke to an empty bed, the sheet and blanket, still damp, wrapped around her legs. The brightness in the room was more orange than usual. It seemed artificial, like stage lights, and she thought for a moment that it had all been a dream, a cruel nightmare. She threw her legs over the side of the bed and planted her feet on the cool floor. Toya shivered. A slight ache in her thighs and back recalled the pre-dawn lovemaking. It had been real. Toya stared down at her feet and listened to the quiet of the apartment. She looked over her shoulder at the place Folami had slept, the twist of sheets and blankets.

Toya had been here before. Frightened of the depth of her feelings or upset, but most certainly disappointed in herself and confused, Folami had probably scooped her clothes off the floor and dressed in the living room before leaving, quietly closing the door and creeping down the stairs. Toya stood up and stretched. She parted the blinds and looked down at the alley below before stepping back to grab her pants off the floor. She slid them on and walked topless through the silent hallway and into the living room.

Folami sat naked, holding her legs against her chest. Her clothes were beside her on the couch. She rested her chin on her knees and hunched her shoulders.

"I didn't want to wake you," she said.

"Are you okay?" Toya asked.

Folami turned her head. "No," she said.

Toya's heart sank.

"I'm hungry," Folami said.

Toya made pancakes and sliced bananas, which they ate with coffee and large glasses of water. They were mostly quiet. The morning seemed too heavy for light conversation but too bright for the weight of their feelings and experiences of the night before, the unfortunate events that led them to the uncertain night, the secret security of their spooning, the surprise of their lovemaking.

BOOK IV

Chapter Sixteen

Toya stood near the door, scanning the room for a place to sit. Three men sat wide-legged and slouched on the sofa, and a collection of men, women, and children filled the metal folding chairs scattered about the living room. Some of the people leaned into each other, small, whispered conversation bouncing between them while others sat silently, staring at their own feet or gazing at the figurines on the mantel. The television, a thirty-two-inch box set flat screen donated to RiseUP! after an unfortunate break-in earlier in the year, sat on a metal cart near the fireplace. The cart had been rolled in from the director's office. Toya squinted at the screen and frowned at the empty podium and scrolling marquee with quick updates and facts on the trial rotated along with football scores, celebrity birthdays, and weather reports.

Folami peeked into the living room from the kitchen. She motioned for Toya to come to her, and she made her way to the back of the house. She noticed the poster board and markers, paint tubes and rulers that littered the dining room table as she made her way to the kitchen. Folami, Fishbone, and Kanaan stood near the sink, arms crossed and whispering to each other.

"Finally," Kanaan said. "I didn't think you were coming."

"Why wouldn't I?" Toya said. She looked past him and smiled at Folami. She smiled back. Toya had put her mother's message way, way back in the recesses of her mind. The divorce had nothing to do with her, and she wasn't interested in helping or being involved in any way at all. Instead, she focused on work and enjoying her time with Folami. They had spent the last few weeks between their two apartments, putting the finishing touches on the videos and planning a visibility event for the neighborhood.

"Just ain't heard from you or seen you since the rally," Kanaan said. "Wasn't sure if you still in your feelings." He shrugged.

"*You* ain't heard from me since the rally," Toya said. She looked over at Fishbone. "Fish," she said and smiled at him, too. He gave her a head nod and quick fist salute.

"Good turnout. The director here?" she asked, taking her camera from around her neck and placing it on the table.

"Yeah," Folami said. "He's in his office. He said come get him when Donovan comes out."

"I see the community is here, the stuff for signs. Folami get y'all up to speed with our visibility idea?" Toya glanced over her shoulder as someone came into the kitchen.

"The attorney's coming in!" a woman in a white, black, and red T-shirt and matching head wrap said without even clearing the doorway. She let the door swing closed before they could even respond.

They all rushed into the living room.

Rick Donovan, the state attorney for Seminole County, shuffled papers at the wooden podium, his face crinkled into a frown and lips pulled tight against his teeth. He smoothed the front of his red and gray tie and looked up into the camera. Brown-eyed with wispy eyebrows and flat, grayish brown hair, a swoop of it combed over his diminishing hairline, Donovan had become a familiar face over the last couple of weeks. Always in a black suit with an American flag pin on his lapel, he smiled uncomfortably during interviews and stretched his neck forward before answering difficult questions. At the podium, he looked to his left and right. Other Seminole County officials stood around him. All of them white except one, a Latino woman with short salt-and-pepper hair and glasses. She and the others—a random collection of forgettable pale faces and dull eyes—stood expressionless with their arms at their sides.

Toya supposed they represented the authority and governance of Evergreen, a small town of a little over fifty thousand people that illustrated perfectly the great division of most American cities and towns. The black and brown people, situated uncomfortably beneath the poverty line, made up most of Evergreen's east side, the side riddled with cheap apartments, liquor stores, and run-down gas stations, the side with no public garbage cans or bus stop shelters, the side with no specialty shops or open air markets. The moneyed in Evergreen, predominantly white, lived on the west side, lakefront properties with blooming magnolias in their backyards, brightly colored bougainvillea winding around painted white trellises.

Attorney Donovan cleared his throat and stretched his neck forward. Toya looked around the room; all eyes were glued to the screen. She turned her attention back to Donovan. He adjusted the gooseneck microphone then gripped the sides of the podium.

"Good afternoon," Donovan said. "We're convening today to release the grand jury decision in the case of the fatal shooting of J'Quan Miles by off-duty officer Eric Vaughn. After a thorough investigation of the facts, the case was presented to a grand jury who, after careful consideration of the facts, and the sworn testimony of Officer Vaughn..." Donovan stretched his neck forward.

Toya held her breath. She couldn't take her eyes off the screen. Folami slipped her hand into Toya's and squeezed. She squeezed back. The house went completely silent. Everyone held their breath.

Donovan cleared his throat and looked down at his papers. Cameras clicked and flashes of blue lit up Donovan's face as he looked over his shoulders at the people standing at his sides. He looked straight ahead, his brown eyes blank and determined as he continued. "The grand jury has considered the facts and the testimony and have decided not to charge Officer Vaughn with involuntary manslaughter, as would be the charge brought by this office. The grand jury has found that a criminal violation could not be proven"—Donovan cleared his throat and stretched his neck—"without a reasonable doubt."

Cries of "Bullshit" and "What the fuck?" shook the room. A man in fatigues and a black T-shirt jumped up and pressed at his temples while repeating "I knew it. I knew it" under his breath. A woman grabbed her daughter, a bony girl with Nubian knots and a Happy to be Nappy tank top, and held her close to her large bosom, tears falling and lips trembling as she kissed the girl's forehead. Kanaan snatched an empty chair and pushed it across the room to the front door, narrowly missing the couple in matching Malcolm X shirts, who sat side-by-side holding each other and crying. Toya's eyes burned. The faces in the room blurred together, ran together like dripping water color. Heat spread across her forehead. Her stomach lurched. Folami still held her hand. She hadn't moved. She hadn't made a sound. Her hand tightened and tightened and tightened. It hurt, the squeezing became a crushing, Toya's knuckles gnashing against each other, Folami's fingers a vice-grip. Toya blinked out quick, hot tears. She looked at Folami. Her eyes wide and unblinking. Her chest neither rising nor falling. Toya tried to squeeze Folami's hand back but couldn't move her fingers.

Someone else pushed a chair. It hit the edge of the sofa then toppled over. Moaning and crying rivaled the cursing and questions. Director Abasi raised his hands to calm everyone down, but nothing changed in the room, voices got louder. "BULLSHIT!" "WHAT THE FUCK?" "CRAZY" and "WHAT

THE FUCK JUST HAPPENED?" More crying, more sniffling, more rocking and teetering chairs. Folami still hadn't moved except to keep squeezing Toya's hand. And it hurt more and more. The pain throbbed from the tips of Toya's fingers to her wrists.

"Brothers and sisters," Director Abasi said. "Brothers and sisters!" He raised his hand again, trying to get people to be quiet. His face tightened into a deep frown, his shoulders flexed underneath his purple and black dashiki. "Settle down now," he said. He reached out and placed a hand on Kanaan's shoulder. Kanaan shrugged it off and kicked at an abandoned chair. Director Abasi grabbed Kanaan by both shoulders and shook him once. "Young brother! Collect yourself!"

At the strong urging of the director's voice, everyone stopped. They turned their attention to Director Abasi, who released Kanaan with a tiny shove. Everyone looked at each other and at the director, everyone except Folami; her eyes were still glued to the screen, still wide and unblinking. Toya didn't notice it at first, especially not with all the shouting and crying, but Folami was making a noise. A low, humming noise. A building noise like a kettle heating up. A low gurgle, a bass-like rumble rose in the back of her throat. Director Abasi reached out to her, but it was too late.

The scream hurt. The shrill ring of it. The sharpness of it. The entire moment fragile as glass, everything and everyone shattered at the sound. Their hopes and dreams, their understanding and resolve, all of it, destroyed by the cry to end all cries.

When Folami finally stopped, the room took on an uncomfortable silence so thick and suffocating, it was a wonder anyone could breathe. Toya reached out to Folami and pulled her into her arms. With her face pressed into the side of Toya's neck, Folami sobbed. Wet. Hot. Heaving sobs. The woman in the head wrap cried, too, her tears falling silently down her pockmarked cheeks. One man held the bridge of his nose while turning away from Toya's gaze; his tears would be private. The children in the room looked frightened and confused. Folami shuddered against Toya while she looked around. Toya rubbed Folami's back then stopped when she caught Kanaan's glare.

"This is that bullshit I'm talking 'bout," Kanaan said. "All this damn crying and sorrow." He scanned the room. He stopped at the man who had turned away from everyone to cry. He and Kanaan stared at each other. "And guilt. Sorrow and guilt. Shame." He spat out the last word.

The man wiped at his eyes.

"This sadness is useless. This guilt." Kanaan shook his head. "The guilt ain't ours. It's theirs. It's always been THEIRS!" he yelled. "When we gonna stop all this goddamn crying and hugging and DO SOMETHING!" He kicked at the toppled over chair at his feet.

"Oh, you big and bad, huh?" Director Abasi said.

Folami stopped crying at the sound of Abasi's voice but kept her face nestled in Toya's neck. She squeezed Toya tight. Toya returned the embrace, holding Folami against her chest.

"What should we do, young brother Kanaan?" Director Abasi asked. "You want to jump in the car and ride up to Evergreen right now? You want to pile in as many brothers with guns and bats as we can and bust up the courthouse? Kill as many white devils as we can?"

"Yeah," Kanaan said. "All of that! ANY OF IT!" He stepped into the center of the room. "Anything is better than standing around crying and hugging and shit while we're murdered without consequence. You said it yourself, Director, BLOOD! BLOOD! BLOOD!"

Folami jumped when Kanaan yelled. She pulled her face from Toya's neck.

Kanaan stared Abasi down. "Or was that just lip service? Just a chant to get people going and get yourself on YouTube? Up there with all them preachers who pimp their own people."

"What did you just call me?" Director Abasi said. He put his hands on his hips and popped his thick neck.

"I ain't call you nothing, but if the podium fits," Kanaan said. He crossed his arms and challenged Director Abasi with his eyes.

Director Abasi smiled. An odd, scary smile. "You got a lot to learn about how a movement works. I've been a soldier in this war since before you could wipe your own ass. Now, I don't want to disrespect you, young brother. I remember when you joined us, and I know more about you than you think I do, more about you than you would be comfortable with."

Toya sensed the argument getting personal when the focus very much needed to stay on what Kanaan was saying. He wasn't completely right, and Toya still couldn't get on board with a rally cry for violence, but he had a point. She closed her eyes, remembering the music, the chant. Blood. Blood. I'm on my way. She decided to speak up.

"So what? We should read more books? Watch more bootleg DVDs?" Toya said. "You've been a soldier in a losing war, Director Abasi. And I say that with the utmost respect for all you've done. But look at what we have. Another murder and another murderer who will not be held accountable. No one is going to pay for it. We die and no one pays for it!" she said.

Folami, Kanaan, and Director Abasi looked at Toya, surprised.

Toya couldn't be silent. Book after book after book. Documentary after documentary after documentary. She looked directly at Folami and found courage in her eyes.

"It's frustrating, Director Abasi. It's frustrating and the shit hurts. It really, really hurts." Tears burned Toya's eyes, but she fought them. She swallowed the lump forming in her throat, forced it down into the fiery pit of her stomach. "We need something else to do other than hold rallies. We need to get in the streets. We need to shut shit down." Toya glanced at Folami again and thought about their discussions over the past week. Lying in bed, playing with each other's hands and talking big as the sky, they came up with an idea for shutting down the city, making a real statement.

"This decision," Dr. Abasi said, "is complete lunacy. We know that. But your anger is misguided. Your frustration without focus. You all seem to be a little too emotional to think clearly. That's evident." He folded his thick, muscular arms across his chest. His biceps bulged and chest inflated. He looked at Folami, Toya, and Kanaan with admonishment and disappointment.

"The decision isn't just lunacy. It's complete bullshit. It's racial profiling at best," Folami said, finally finding her voice. She looked at Director Abasi, and he took in more air, inflating himself even more against the voices of dissension. He was like a pot set to boil.

"He looked like he was going to break into a house?" Fishbone said. "Based on what?"

"I want to hear Vaughn's testimony," Folami said.

"I don't," Kanaan said. "I don't need to hear it. Fuck him and his testimony. He saw a Black man walking and cut a Black man down. He can say whatever the fuck he wants and get away with the shit."

"Dead men tell no tales," Toya said.

Kanaan nodded at Toya and a few other people in the room joined in, nodding and commenting among themselves.

"It's, like, what year is it?" the woman in the head wrap said. She looked at Kanaan as she stood up.

"Might as well be the damn fifties!" the man who had hid his tears said. "Are those the times you talking about, Director Abasi? Over sixty fucking years ago?!"

"Watch your language with these babies in here," Director Abasi said. "I get it. You all are angry. I know. But you have to direct it. Use it. We can't dismantle a system without a clear vision of what to do next. Who wins with a city in ruins? Who wins with bodies in the street?" He looked at Kanaan. "Yeah, I called for blood. And the metaphor should be clear. The life-blood of the system is power, young brother. POWER. That's what we're after." Director Abasi clenched his fist and shook it at Kanaan. He turned and nodded to everyone else in the room, holding his fist at chest level, his forearm and bicep flexing. "Power, brothers and sisters. Political, economic, and social POWER!"

Kanaan sighed. He looked at Toya and Folami. He smirked at the woman in the head wrap before turning his attention back to Director Abasi. Kanaan put a hand to his chest and lowered his voice. "I'm not interested in no fucking metaphors."

Director Abasi's fist clenched once more. From the way he stared at Kanaan, Toya thought he would coldcock him and lay him right out on the floor. The room fell silent.

Toya spoke up, becoming a mediator of sorts. Both Kanaan and Director Abasi had valid points. Nothing seemed to be changing in the midst of marching and rallies, but on the other hand, anarchy would solve nothing, help no one.

"Director Abasi," Toya said. "You gotta give us something. If you're leading us, you gotta give us something more than speeches and history. The work of our ancestors is important, but we gotta build on it, not repeat it."

Director Abasi chuckled and shook his head. "Young brothers and sisters, you're free to do whatever you like. Always. But I challenge you to think it through. And when you're ready, really ready, to claim victory, to take power, I'll see you back here."

"Whatever," Kanaan said. He cleared his throat and moved toward the door. He stopped before opening it, his hand resting on the knob. He turned to face everyone. "I'm sure y'all about to start talking, and while you're talking, you'll make your way to that table over there and get to making signs and banners and shit." He shook his head. He bent at the waist and directed his attention to the little girl sitting with her mother. She wore coveralls and a green T-shirt, her hair in two fluffy afro puffs. "There's lots of pretty colors over there for you to play with," Kanaan said. He smiled at the girl and her mother. The mother cut her eyes. He stood up. "For those of y'all *not* interested in playing with markers and crayons, I'm having a meeting at midnight tonight. Ask Fish for details." Kanaan yanked open the door and left.

Fishbone turned at the mention of his name, a look of surprise on his slender, scruffy face. He had been sitting in a chair in the dining room. He had a pen and legal pad in front of him, and other than him snapping his fingers every so often as he scribbled away, Toya had forgotten he was even there.

"I don't want to sit through another lecture," Folami said as Director Abasi disappeared into his office and closed the door. "I want to do something. I need to do something." She blinked back tears as she spoke. "You coming?" she asked.

Toya looked over her shoulder at Fishbone, who swiped up his pad and pen and headed toward the kitchen, where he would more than likely slink out the back door.

"Yeah," Toya said. She and Folami stepped through the front room, the people there talking among themselves and hugging through their tears.

Once outside on the porch, Toya stopped and grabbed Folami's arm. "I agree that we need to do something, Folami," she said. "But I'm not down with Kanaan like that. He's talking about hurting people. He's talking about vengeance. I'm mad. I'm enraged. I'm hurt. But this movement has got to be about love. At its core, it's got to be about love. Not murder. Not revenge."

Folami sighed. "I know. And the things we've talked about have been great. I'm all about the multi-faceted approach and the whole shutting shit down. I really like your plan. Maybe we can sell Kanaan on it. Maybe we can get him to bring some of his crew over to our side."

Toya thought about the way Kanaan looked at her and Folami inside the house. She wondered if Folami had come out and told him about their relationship. "I don't know that we need his crew. I don't know that they would even want to work with us."

"I'm going to give them the benefit of the doubt," Folami said. "We gotta try. We need all the help we can get."

"I don't know, Folami."

"I do," she said. "Trust me."

Toya sighed. "You go. Come by later and tell me about it?"

Folami smiled at Toya's uncertainty. She leaned over and kissed her on the cheek.

Chapter Seventeen

Toya, in oversized jogging pants and a sports bra, lay stretched out on the couch staring at the Fannie Lou Hamer poster and willing Folami to arrive. It had been hours. When Folami left, Toya had gone back in the house to get her camera and found Fishbone still inside. They sat together at the table as Director Abasi had gone into a brief history of the police and their function as slave-wranglers, checking for freed men's papers being their primary task at their inception. The talk was interesting, and when he brought it to current day, so much of the anger and confusion we all felt had context.

After the talk, Fishbone read the poem he had written to the few people who had decided to stay. Toya decided to share some of her ideas for the visibility event with the women and children who hung around to make signs, and ended up losing herself in the markers and paint, stickers and tape.

The knocks were soft, a hollow rap of Folami's knuckles against the wood. Toya jumped up and opened the door.

"I didn't want to wake you," Folami said. "I know it's really late."

"I wasn't asleep," Toya said. "Come inside."

Folami entered the apartment, her face bright and energetic in a way Toya didn't quite expect. Her eyes danced, and she seemed on the verge of a smile.

Folami made her way to the couch, and Toya went to the kitchen area.

Toya grabbed herself a water. "Can I get you—"

"Oh my God, Toya! You should have been there!" Folami said.

Toya came out of the kitchen. Folami jumped up and started talking with her hands. "Kanaan's meeting was crazy! So many people for one! So many new faces down for the struggle, you know? There were some brothers there who you would never think in a million years would be down for community activism! I mean, they looked like straight up bangers. But they were so down. So ready. And some of the sisters who came I've never seen before, and they were ready too. The conversation was so dope, so full of fresh ideas, so full of...of...fire!"

Toya nodded. "Well, that...that sounds like something."

"It was everything, Toya. Everything." Folami sat down. "Kanaan has this friend from North Carolina who just got here today. His name is Supreme Self."

"Wait, his name is what?"

"Supreme Self." Folami shook her head. "I know, a little pretentious."

"A little?"

"His name ain't the point, Toya." She slapped playfully at Toya's hand. "This man was...he was giving voice to all of our frustrations. All of our anger. Black Wall Street in Tulsa, Rosewood right here in Florida, and more, so many more. A history of destroying our communities. And what? What do we do? March? Have vigils? He was talking about action. He was talking about taking it to the streets."

"Taking what to the streets? You on that violent shit like Kanaan now?" Toya sighed and pushed herself back on the couch.

"Damn it, Toya. This isn't about Kanaan." Folami frowned and stood up again.

"I know it's not…" Toya said. "It's about what he represents. He's this…He's…"

"He's a man," Folami said. "Is that the problem?"

"What? Hell no." Toya stood up too. "It has nothing to do with him being a man. How could you say that?"

"It's not unbelievable to me," Folami said. "I know you have your problems with him, but I just don't see what you see."

"Are you kidding?" Toya said. "Let me ask you a question. Did you tell him about us?"

"What?"

"You heard me. Did you tell him about us?"

Folami sighed. "This ain't about that, Toya." She waved her hand dismissively.

"You haven't," Toya said. "You still don't get it. Do you?"

"I get it more than you think," Folami said. She walked over to the Fannie Lou Hamer poster and ran her finger along the bottom of the frame. "I'm not talking about gender politics, Toya. I'm not talking about sexuality. I'm not talking about the way Kanaan looked at me like I was the scum of the earth when he asked if you and I were sleeping together and I answered his question honestly." She exhaled. "I'm not talking about him. I'm talking about moving my people. I'm talking about reaching hearts and heads whatever way we can." Folami stared at Fannie then turned to Toya.

Toya walked over to her. "We live at an intersection, Folami. We gotta move in multiple directions, not just one."

"It's not multiple directions," Folami said. Her voice softened. "It's one direction. Forward."

"Well then, we all have the right to go," Toya said. "We all have the right to move forward."

"Look, RiseUP! doesn't have all the answers. Neither does Kanaan…or even Supreme Self. There's so much more. We're part of that more." Folami took Toya's hand.

"More," Toya said.

"More," Folami repeated. "We're about to do so much more."
She leaned in and kissed Toya. Toya kissed her back.

Toya imagined them then, the two of them, invigorating a new movement. A movement full of fire and energy. A freshness to the work. Signs and marching, group workshops and community meetings, teach-ins at the grade schools and media campaigns. Everything they were already doing, yet even more of it; things they had yet to do and even more of that. Toya knew it would be a lot of work, but she was ready. With Folami, she was ready for anything. Ready for everything.

CHAPTER EIGHTEEN

Toya made sure every hand held a sign or a flag. Folami had found these miniature American flags redesigned in red, black, green, and gold. The thirteen stripes alternate bars of blood and earth, the black square a contrast of skin boasting the richness of fifty golden stars. The smiling faces of young girls and boys waving the tiny flags were enough to make Toya believe in a better tomorrow, even as the signs hoisted by the adults screamed out injustices and called out demands for retribution.

So far, the visibility rally Toya and Folami had organized was going well. Toya coordinated groups of people at each corner of the intersection at South Eighteenth Avenue and Sixteenth Street. The "Honk for Justice" and "Blow Your Horns if Black Lives Matter" signs encouraged passing motorists to get involved in the community demonstration. Folami, in a yellow maxi dress and denim vest, the pockets and panels painted with asymmetrical red, black, and green shapes, handed out flyers and engaged with people at the convenience store. She caught customers as they entered and as they left, smiling with encouragement and frowning with concern depending on the receptiveness of the patrons.

Toya nodded in Folami's direction when she caught her staring, and the smile she gave made Toya stand up straighter. She lifted her hands to the camera around her neck and zoomed in to Folami as she handed a flyer each to a group of young boys who had rolled up on their bikes.

Toya smiled at her once more before turning her attention to capturing a few shots of the people on the corners. Car horns exploded in short bursts and long blasts as people shook their signs at the passing traffic, raising their fists and yelling out "No justice! No peace!" and "We will not be moved!"

After snapping a few more shots, Toya made her way over to the convenience store to ask Folami for the keys to the car. More people than they anticipated showed up, and though they had run out of hand-painted signs, they still had plenty of African-themed American flags in the trunk of the Impala.

"Can you believe this turnout?" Toya asked as she walked up to Folami. She capped her camera lens and glanced over her shoulder at the crowded intersections.

"Actually, I can," Folami said. "People are still upset about the non-indictment. Something is happening, Toya. It's a fever pitch. And we're right where we need to be." She smiled proudly, bumping Toya's shoulder then handing a flyer to two women as they walked into the store.

"This is just the beginning," Toya said. She dug into the duffel bag at Folami's feet and grabbed a stack of flyers. "I'll hand these out on my way to the car. Let me get the keys. We need more flags."

"Give me some flyers, too," a low, velvet smooth voice said from behind Toya's back.

Toya looked at Folami, whose face crinkled in confusion and challenge, before she turned.

"Billie Holiday!" Toya said, pulling Nina into an enthusiastic one-armed hug. Her camera jostled between them. She steadied it quickly. "What are you doing here?"

Nina beamed and put her arm around Toya. "My friend Taylor is from here, and so we decided to come down before heading back up to Atlanta. We've been in Evergreen for a few weeks."

"What's the vibe like up there since the decision?" Toya asked.

"It's quiet but tense," she said. She furrowed her eyebrows; the sun glinted off the round frames of her sunglasses. "We'd been super-amped up since the rally and even had a demonstration the day of the announcement. It was like five hundred of us outside that courthouse. It was beeeeeeeeeautiful! When the word came back nil, we lost it. We stayed out there all night and into the next day. Immovable, yo."

Toya nodded and smiled. "That's amazing," she said.

"But you know, the days wore on and folks slowly went back to their lives. A few of us stayed on, organizing small sit-ins and still mobbin' the courthouse steps. And we—"

Folami cleared her throat.

"Oh shit," Toya said. "Folami, this is Billie—I mean, Nina. This is Nina." She chuckled through the correction. Nina tightened her arm around Toya's neck and bumped her with the round of her small hip. "Nina, this is Folami."

Folami held out her hand. Nina slid her arm from around Toya and took Folami's hand in both of hers. She shook it once then held it.

"I remember you from the Miles rally," Nina said.

Folami smiled a tight-lipped smile. "That's right." She slid her hand out from Nina's grip and placed it on her hip. She looked at Toya and gave her that same flat smile.

"Here," Toya said. She gave Nina a stack of flyers. "You want more?"

"Yeah," she said. She glanced over her shoulder. "I've got a few folks with me. I'll give them some. We'll canvas this whole zip code!" she said the last with a giggle that was equal parts mischief and humor.

The sound contagious, Toya laughed too. She looked at Folami. Another forced, phony smile. Folami turned her attention to a group of girls laughing and juggling bags of chips, canned pops, and candy in their skinny arms.

Toya knew jealousy when she saw it. It amused her that Folami would be jealous of this woman she barely knew, yet it thrilled her all the same. She and Folami, though not loving exactly in secret anymore, hadn't really talked about an official relationship status. They had decided to focus on the work, dedication to the movement the only real promise between them.

"Actually," Toya said. "I should give you some flags to hand out, too." She handed Nina another small stack of palm card flyers and tapped Folami on the shoulder.

"What's up?" Folami said coolly.

"The keys? I'm going to get more flags," Toya said.

Folami went into her vest pocket and produced the keys. She dropped them into Toya's outstretched hand. "You remember where it's parked?"

Toya nodded. "Nina's gonna walk over there with me. I'm gonna give her some flags, too." She grinned.

"Yup," Folami said and turned.

Toya looked at Nina, who shrugged and smiled.

Nina leaned against a tree, flicking her thumb through the flyers to create a private breeze. Toya shifted empty boxes around in the trunk and finally found the cloth shopping bag full of miniature flags.

"Your friend doesn't like me," Nina said.

Toya smirked as she hoisted the over-stuffed bag from the trunk.

"Or maybe she's your girlfriend and that's why," she said. "Hmm mmm. That makes the most sense," she answered her own question. "Protective, huh?"

Toya dropped the bag and looked at her. "What?"

Nina smiled and pushed herself from the tree. She reached over to help Toya pull the bag up and out of the trunk. They set it on the bumper. Nina smelled like talcum powder and rosewater, soothing and sweet.

"Your girlfriend, Folami," Nina said. "She's obviously the jealous type."

"Folami isn't my girlfriend," Toya said. She frowned. She didn't like the way the sentiment sounded coming out of her mouth. She said it again, "Folami isn't my girlfriend," as if the second time would make it feel better, soften the hard truth.

"Does she know that?" Nina's eyes pressed, prying for more context. She stood close to Toya. Their arms touched as Toya shifted the bag onto her thighs to better bunch up the thin wooden sticks that made up the flagpoles.

"I mean, we're close but..." Toya stopped.

Nina smiled knowingly. She licked her lips. "Oh, I see. It's complicated?" She laughed.

"No. But, yes. Hey, Folami's a suspicious person in general. Always on guard." Toya lied, covering for Folami. They'd talk about it later, the jealousy, the rudeness, and what it meant.

"If she ain't your girlfriend, she wants to be," Nina said.

Toya steadied the bag and gripped a handful of flags. She pushed the flags down and situated the handles of the bag then slid it onto her shoulder. "Why are we even talking about this?" Toya said.

"Hey, just forget I said anything," Nina said, raising her hands in surrender. She bit her bottom lip and made eye contact before she looked Toya up and down, lingering at her thighs then her mouth.

Toya cleared her throat. "Come on, woman. Let's head back."

Toya and Nina walked back to the intersection. She told her a little bit about the area. The multiple generations of families who lived in the old shotgun houses and block homes. She talked about the storefronts and backyard hustles—Mr. Redd's barbecue, Ms. Janie's alterations, Wanda's Child Care. Businesses run out of their homes, hand-painted signs stuck in the sparse grass of their front yards.

When they reached the intersection, the first thing they noticed was a black, Ford F-250 XLT, the tailgate extended and a small group of men standing in the bed. Toya recognized Kanaan and Fishbone right away. They wore all black, Kanaan in his mirrored sunglasses, his dreads stuffed into a red, black, and green knit hat and Fishbone's knotty dreads piled high on his head with a pencil sticking out the side. She didn't know the other two men, but assumed the tall, slender man with the cropped haircut and neatly lined facial hair had to be Supreme Self. He wore a brown sleeveless shirt, white adinkra symbols embroidered along the hem and neckline, and white linen pants. His toned arms, free of tattoos but scarred with the raised, deep brown contours of Afrika burned onto one shoulder and a Greek symbol burned onto the other, flexed as he clapped along with the chanting crowd across from the convenience store where Folami had stood. She had moved across the street, and Toya spotted her leaning against the traffic signal, her eyes bright and jubilant.

"Who's that?" Nina asked.

"Supreme Self," Toya said.

She laughed. "For real?"

Toya nodded and pursed her lips. "That's what I said."

They walked across the street and joined Folami at the traffic signal post. She smiled at both of them and returned her attention to the truck. One of the men Toya didn't know bent down and produced a bullhorn. He hit the siren button to get everyone's attention and to quiet the chanting. He greeted everyone with "Hotep" and asked everyone how they were feeling. People clapped and nodded, yelled out "all right" and "I'm feeling good!" He cleared his throat into the microphone, the phlegmy gurgle echoing against the murmurs of the crowd. He turned to Fishbone and nodded before introducing him as "Lyrical Freedom."

Fishbone grabbed the bullhorn and held it to his chest with his eyes closed. He swayed in a personal wind, a breeze no one but him could feel, and he licked his brown lips, baring his yellowed teeth with something like a wincing smile. He brought the microphone to his lips and rambled off a rhythmic verse of double entendres and metaphors, similes and personifications— freedom as a woman left to die on a railroad track and oppression as an acid rain that burned hieroglyphics into flesh. When he finished, he opened his eyes and surveyed the crowd before kissing his fingertips, pounding his chest with his open palm, then raising his fist over his head.

The crowd cheered and applauded. Toya settled the bag of flags at her feet and quickly took the lens cap from her camera. She snuck a few quick shots of Fishbone with his fist raised and eyes to the sky before dropping the camera to clap her hands.

Fishbone handed the bullhorn off to the stranger, a short, squat brother with a receding hairline and a dingy, ribbed white tank top stretched across his potbelly. He coughed into the microphone and cleared his throat.

"Brothers and sisters, are you ready?" he said.

Toya leaned into Folami to whisper in her ear. "You knew about this?"

She shook her head. "I was handing out flyers and they just pulled up, honking the horn and blasting Fela. Everyone crowded around and then…this." She gestured toward the truck.

The man cleared his throat again then raised a hand to calm down the clapping and cheering of the crowd.

"Brothers and sisters, it is my honor and my pleasure, my esteemed privilege and utmost excitement, to present to you, for you and your third eye, get your mind right, raise them fists! It's SUPREME SELF!"

The man handed the bullhorn off to Supreme Self, who held it against his chest and rested his chin on the mic. The crowd clapped, and as their applause died down, he raised his fist, and the audience picked back up with enthusiastic responses of both clapping and chanting "Black Power."

Supreme Self lifted the microphone and yelled into the air. "THIS MEANS WAR!"

The crowd clapped and nodded.

"And I'm not talking merely about the obvious and heinous murder of our young brothers. The blood overrunning the streets is but one thing. Our Black men have been, and are currently, under assault from multiple fronts. The blows have been many, the shots fired have been carefully aimed, and what's more, what's more, is that they know that when you destroy the Black man, you destroy the Black family, and if you destroy the Black family, you destroy Black people."

Folami nodded. And clapped. She nodded and clapped. When Toya looked at her, she shrugged and clapped.

Having finally gotten a chance to see the man Folami had come to the apartment all hyped up and inspired by, Toya had to say she was disappointed. Supremely disappointed. In Folami. Toya glanced over at Nina, whose eyes had already sharpened and hardened, her face already nonplussed.

"Another one of these," Nina said through clenched teeth. "I know where this is going, and I'm not staying around for it." She raised herself on her toes and searched the crowd for her friends.

"The entirety of the Black race is on the brink of extinction. One Black man at a time. One Black family at a time." Supreme Self stepped forward on the truck bed and put a foot on the edge of the truck. He leaned over at the waist, his eyes glowing hazel, his eyebrows thick but neat, his teeth even and white. A small goatee framed his full pink lips. Flawless skin, symmetrical features. He was almost beautiful. He narrowed his eyes and snarled, an attempt to become the rage he needed to project to the crowd.

"I'm going to go," Nina said.

"Wait," Toya said. She placed a hand on Nina's arm. Two of her friends, a Black boy who looked like he could have been her brother, his hair cut into a blond Mohawk, and a thin white boy whose brown hair swirled around his head in a thick mess of waves and spikes, walked up beside her. She handed them the flags and flyers. Folami glanced over at them before turning her attention back to the truck and the accusatory glare of Supreme Self. His honey eyes, more searing than sweet, scanned the crowd then stopped on them.

"This is war!" he whispered into the megaphone. "The worst kind of war," he said, even and calm. "We are under siege. They come for us with bullets, reducing us to corpses. They come for us with faggots, reducing us to effeminate pussycats that can't protect our women and children!" He raised a finger in our direction. "THIS IS WAR!"

Applause, not as enthusiastic as before but energetic enough to unnerve Toya as she looked around the crowd. A few "Amens" and a couple "That's rights" flew up and over their heads, the cosigning like bird shit raining down on Toya's, Folami's, and Nina's heads. Toya stood stunned and angry. She looked to Folami, and when she returned her stare, apology and shame lived in her eyes. Apology and shame. Neither of which Toya saw when she glanced over her shoulder at Nina, whose eyes mirrored her own. Anger lived there. Anger and hurt.

"I knew it," Nina said. "I'm outta here." She elbowed the slender white boy and nodded at her brother. "Let's go. We don't need this shit."

"The homosexual agenda continues to make a mockery of our families, and what's worse, continues to ever confuse and confound our sense of identity as Afrikans, our sense of self. Our sense of supreme self." Supreme Self paused for a moment, as if ruminating on his own name, venerating himself as one and all, a great consciousness of everyone in attendance. He stood up straight, watching Nina and her friends turning to leave. "A Black man with no use for the Black woman is the beginning of the end, and the Black woman with no use for the Black man is the very epitome of treachery."

"Folami," Toya said. "You hear this bullshit?"

"I hear him," she said, rolling her eyes. "I didn't know he would be talking about—"

"Peace, Queens," Kanaan said, hopping off the back of the truck and walking up to Toya and Folami.

"Kanaan, what the fuck is this bullshit?" Toya said.

"Bullshit? I don't hear any bullshit." He shrugged and looked at Folami then Toya.

"That's all I've been hearing," Toya said. "Me and Folami organized this event and then you gon' bum-rush it with this hateful, WRONG ass shit!?"

The man with the phlegm got back on the megaphone and introduced Fishbone again. Supreme Self hopped off the truck and joined Folami, Kanaan, and Toya.

"There a problem, sista?" Supreme Self said, walking up on Toya. He challenged her with his smoldering honey eyes.

"Yeah," Toya said. "There's a big problem."

Supreme Self stood up and inflated his chest. He furrowed his brow and tilted his head in mock concern. "I'd love to hear you out, sista. From the looks of things, you might be confused yourself. And it's like I told brother Kanaan the other night, I'm here to help." He smiled. A salesman smile. A slick, serpentine smile.

"We don't need your fucking help!" Toya said.

A small crowd began to form around them. Folami put her hand on Toya's arm and gripped it. "Don't," she said.

Toya yanked her arm from Folami's hand. "Don't?" Toya said. She twisted her face at Folami and shook her head. "Fuck that. Fuck him! Fuck this nigga!"

Kanaan's eyes grew wide at Toya's exclamation. Supreme Self chuckled and looked around at the small group of people who had crowded around their scene.

"So I'm a nigga?" Supreme Self said. He smiled at Toya and rested his hands behind him like a church usher. "You using the language of the oppressor now?"

"What?" Toya said. She looked at him then to Folami. The look on her face made Toya sick. Folami's eyes pleaded for her to stop, for her to be quiet, to let it go. The glaring eyes of a mother whose child was making a scene in the grocery store.

"Fuck you, you, and you!" Toya said, pointing at Kanaan, Supreme Self, and Folami. "Fuck all of this," she said. Toya kicked the bag of flags and turned. The crowd clapped along with the beat Fishbone made on his bony chest and Toya pushed through them, calling out Nina's name.

Chapter Nineteen

Toya; Nina; Ray, the boy who turned out to be her cousin and not her brother; and the white boy, Taylor, sat at a picnic table at Chattaway's, a small restaurant on South Fourth Street with an outside dining area hidden from the street. The other tables were mostly empty. Having just missed the lunch rush, the place was quiet and serene, the light trickle of water in the koi pond and soft seventies music playing in the background accented the slight breeze and warm sun.

"I should have followed my first mind," Nina said. "I knew the second you told me that fool's name that he was going to be some fake-intellectual-Hotep-asshole." She shrugged and contemplated the menu.

"He reminded me of that one conference, Nina," Ray said. He pursed his lips before sipping his ice water with lemon. "You remember? You got invited to that panel only to get attacked by the very people who asked you to come!" He shook his head and sipped at his water.

"What happened?" Toya asked. She ran her fingers up and down the sides of her plastic cup, the condensation racing from rim to table, the ice in her unsweetened tea losing to the afternoon sun.

Nina sighed. She looked up at Toya. "Last year, I got invited to speak at a conference."

"Art as Responsibility," Ray said.

"Yeah," Nina said. "The Art as Responsibility Conference. I was a panelist for this session about visual art. I paint and sculpt and do all sorts of mixed media, but with this really socially conscious, humanist aesthetic, right?"

Toya nodded. She brought her tea to her lips. Upset and frustrated, Toya drank the tea in large gulps. She needed the tea to cool her. She still burned hot inside from the encounter with Supreme Self and Kanaan, still boiled with frustration from Folami's response—or more accurately, lack thereof. The tea and the serenity of Chattaway's slowly worked magic. She set her tea down and glanced around as Nina continued. Only a couple of miles away from the rally site, the quaint, colorful restaurant made her feel as if she were on the other side of the world.

"So, it was me and three other artists. Two painters and one other sculptor, two men and one other woman. I felt good about the dynamic, the energy. I liked most of the woman's work, and though I wasn't a hundred percent familiar with the men's work, I knew they wouldn't be on the panel if their work didn't take a decidedly empowering, socio-political stance, right?"

"The one dude painted Black Jesus figures in outer space," Ray said with a roll of his movie star eyes, almond-shaped with long, curled lashes.

"I liked those paintings," Nina said. "Jesus reimagined and placed in this Afro-futuristic collection of quasars and galaxies. Really complex," she said as if trying to convince Ray of the art's value. He shrugged and sipped his water.

"Afro-futuristic as a term always makes me think of some funky cyborg superhero with an electric, purple afro and golden cape." Taylor giggled. Other than pointing at the pond and exclaiming his love of koi fish when they walked across the foot bridge at Chattaway's entrance, it was only the second time Toya had heard his voice.

"Taylor, please," Ray said.

"But you know what I mean, right?" he said. He looked at Toya. "What does 'Afro-futurist' make you think of?"

"Octavia Butler," Toya said.

"Who?" he said with a frown.

"Ignore him," Ray said. "So, Nina gets invited to be on this panel of artists." He talked with his hands, excited to move the story along. "The moderator, this really cute girl with a short cut and the tightest little body. I was thinking Nina should totally try to find out her situation…" He bumped Nina's shoulder and held up a hand to whisper to Toya. "She so picky. That's why she doesn't get laid nearly enough."

Taylor burst into laughter and held his hand up for Ray to slap him a five.

"Would you two shut the fuck up?" Nina said. "The moderator was cute, but she was part of the damn problem." She cut her eyes at her cousin and their friend then turned her attention to Toya.

Nina cleared her throat and began again. "I'm on this panel and it's going well…at first. Really great questions about where we show our work, why our work is important, who our influences are and all that."

"Yeah," Toya said. She leaned in, resting her elbows on the table.

"So, the talk is going well, lively discussion, then the moderator opens it up for audience questions." Nina glanced at Ray.

"That's when it got nasty," Ray said. He pointed at his menu then reached over and pointed at Taylor's menu. They shared a smile.

Nina continued, "First question from the audience, right up-fucking-front, was this woman, a fellow artist whose work I like, and she asked me, specifically asked me—"

"Do you think homosexuality is a particularly Afro-futurist paradigm?" Ray said in a nasal, mocking voice.

"What?!" Toya said, eyes wide with shock.

"Yes, hunty!" Ray said. "Dis-re-spect-ful!"

Nina shook her head. "I wish I were lying. I was absolutely mortified! Then she said, as if I didn't understand the question—"

"Bitch said, 'Homosexuality does nothing to contribute to the progeny and perpetuation of our people,' like a muthafucka needed clarification about what the fuck she was getting at!" Ray snapped.

"Right there at the art talk?" Toya blinked in disbelief. "What did you do?" she said.

"I tried to respond, but so many people stood with her, asking the same kind of ignorant ass, offensive questions, that I had no choice but to leave." Nina shrugged. "I fought my tears, barely raised my head, and hauled ass as people talked about homosexuality as some kind of mental defect. Bitch must have been Cress Welsing's granddaughter or something. Ray walked me out of there. Some of the people were yelling after me. It was so...so..." She stopped. Her eyes welled, but she blinked the tears away, wiping at her eyes and looking across the restaurant to the crude parking lot. She shook her shoulders as if shaking the memory off her very body.

Ray put an arm around her, his face full of the same concern he probably had then. "I got her out of there as quick as I could. The shit was heinous. Completely and totally heinous. Evil," he said. He pulled Nina toward him and kissed her temple.

Nina exhaled. "Anyway, that asshole this afternoon is on that same bullshit. And I just don't have time for it. I'm not here for any of that divisive bullshit."

The server came up, a young college kid with sandy-blond hair and a tight T-shirt. Both Ray and Taylor gave him an appreciative glance before looking down at their menus.

"You guys all set?"

"Yeah," Nina said. "We're ready."

They ordered lunch, and in less than twenty minutes, the table was filled with sweet potato fries and burgers, fried fish and coleslaw.

They ate with an easy, good-natured relaxation that until that moment, Toya hadn't even realized she had missed. She had been so tense the last few weeks, working with Folami and trying to navigate the shortcomings of RiseUP! and the larger community, in addition to dealing with her and Folami's own shortcomings. The mess of things they made sleeping with each other again, the mess that was made of their first event that very afternoon.

"What are you going to do?" Nina asked. She brought her beer to her lips. Toya watched her drink, a soft sheen of sweat at her hairline and clinging to her throat.

"I guess I'm going to go home," Toya said with a shrug.

"You gonna talk to Folami? See where she's sitting with all this? With the so-called special guest?" She put her beer down and licked her lips.

"I don't think I'm ready to talk to her just yet," Toya said. She picked at the half-eaten burger in front of her.

Nina nodded. "Did she know that Supreme Asshole was going to be speaking?"

"She said she didn't," Toya said.

"You believe her?"

"I don't know."

Nina pressed her lips together and wiped her hands on a napkin. "You should come with us," she said.

"Where y'all going?" Toya asked.

"Outer space," Nina said with a mischievous smile. "To take root among the stars."

Toya smiled at the Butler reference. "You know what? That sounds like exactly what I need."

Chapter Twenty

The ride to Taylor's house introduced Toya to a part of St. Petersburg she'd never seen. The brick streets, perfectly manicured lawns, and fancy palm bushes of Old Southeast caught her off guard. When she worked at the Harbordale YMCA, a plain, yellow-painted block building full of the sweetest, toughest children in the world, she never knew that under a mile east of the glass-ridden streets, row houses with broken down porches, and crowded apartment buildings with no AC was one of the neatest, most peaceful neighborhoods in the area.

The houses, columns and fountains, professional landscaping and balconies, blocked the view of the bay from the street, but when they got to Taylor's parents' house, a dreamy pink and white mini-mansion with beveled columns and dwarf palms lining the clean, slate gray paver walkway, Toya got a chance to see the hidden treasure of a view.

"Come on," Nina said. She took Toya's hand and led her through the living room—oversized leather furniture, heavy mahogany tables, oddly-shaped amber glass centerpieces, and large, abstract paintings in thick, carved brass frames filled the space between the foyer and the back patio. Nina slid the door open and pulled her outside.

"Damn," Toya said.

The modest skyscrapers of downtown St. Petersburg stood in the distance, and in the foreground, the flat, calm, shimmering blue of the bay. The decked out patio with simple but elegant furniture complemented the view, and beyond the patio, a clean, calm, kidney-shaped pool reflected the watercolor sky. The richness of the house didn't impress her; the gaudy, clunky style of the rich never excited her. The house reminded her a little bit of her parents' house. Her mother, taking decorative inspiration from glossy magazines full of confusing centerpieces, fake trunks, and nautical tools, never failed to clutter a room with expensive and recognizable, dull and ugly, nods to *Traditional Home* magazine. And though the view of Lake Michigan from her parents' balcony and the patio off the kitchen was breathtaking in its own right, something about the Bay seemed magical in ways the lake only hinted at. It seemed more hopeful somehow, more full of possibility. Maybe because it had never been frozen, never been hard and barren looking like those lonely winters in Milwaukee. She thought then of her mother, about her message. It occurred to her in that moment that her mother could lose her lifestyle, her way of life. All Toya's memories and anger were tied up in her parents' collective actions, and she hadn't thought about what a divorce would mean for her mother. She had been doing well not to think about it. It wasn't her problem. She had to remember that it wasn't her problem.

"You want a drink?" Ray said, joining Toya and Nina on the patio. He held a snifter a quarter full of something honey-colored and fragrant. He sashayed past Toya and Nina and took a seat on the low, L-shaped teak sectional on the right side of the patio, an unlit fire pit ready and patiently waiting for the evening's festivities. On the opposite side of the patio, two lounge chairs flanked an in-ground Jacuzzi.

"Dope, right?" Nina said. "Have a seat. I'll get us some drinks."

Toya joined Ray on the sectional.

"She likes you," Ray said. He sniffed at his cognac.

"Oh yeah?" Toya said. "How do you know?"

Ray threw his head back and laughed. "You stupid or just dumb?"

Toya chuckled. "I can tell, but I wondered how you knew. If she said anything. I don't know what she wants from me." She shrugged.

"To fuck," he said. He sipped his drink slow and watched Toya's face.

Toya raised her eyebrows. "Wow. I thought you said she was really picky and rarely got laid. She doesn't even know me. Not really," she said.

"Nina is picky, but she also has a way of sifting through bullshit quick, fast, and in a hurry. When she's got a good feeling about someone, she's very...about the moment." Ray swirled his drink in his glass then looked over his shoulder to gaze out at the water.

Toya looked out at the water, too. Nina came out carrying two Collins glasses filled with ice, muddled mint leaves, and the unmistakable clarity of good rum. Taylor followed close behind her with a tray of fruit, cheese, crackers, and two expertly rolled blunts. Nina handed Toya a mojito and sat beside her.

"Thank you," Toya said. She lifted her glass; Nina and Ray did the same. Taylor picked up a cigar and held it in the air like a cocktail.

"To..." Nina began.

"The moment," Ray said, winking at Toya before bringing his drink to his lips.

"The moment," Nina, Taylor, and Toya said in unison.

The mojito was absolute perfection, and its tart, minty deliciousness only increased with each refill. Before Toya knew it, night drew near. The sky swelled with cotton candy thunderheads; the sun, sunken and out of sight in the western skies, cast glowing oranges and pinks across the bay. Taylor and Ray had gone inside, the blunt they'd shared sending them into a fit of giggles then an awkward silence where they sat playing with each other's fingers and struggling to keep their eyes open. Nina smoked the remaining cigar. She toyed with the musky-sweet smoke, a reverse waterfall from her mouth to her nose, then swirling, curling, tendrils framing her face.

"You don't smoke?" Nina asked again.

"No," Toya said. "I never really got into it."

Nina nodded. She licked her lips and sat up to put her empty glass on the table beside her. She ashed the blunt, took another long pull, then stubbed it out in the ceramic ashtray near the tray of half-eaten fruit and cheese.

"You've been quiet since we left Chattaway's," she said. "What's the matter?"

"Nothing," Toya said.

"You're lying," Nina said. "But, if you don't want to say, I'm fine with that."

"It's not anything I want to talk about. So, yeah, I don't want to say." Toya leaned back in her seat. She stared at the fire pit, the dancing flames, the crackling hickory and glowing chips of mesquite.

"Check it," Nina said. She put her hand on Toya's thigh. "I don't stand for no bullshit. I'm a humanist, right? I'm about the connected oppression of all those who are oppressed. I fight for all this shit. So, that dude from earlier? Fuck him. And fuck anyone who thinks that fucker is 'droppin' knowledge' and enlightening anyone." She shook her head. "I'm not here for it. Any of it. So fuck it."

"Fuck it is right," Toya said. "I was just so mad because... the ridiculousness of it aside, where the hell did it come from? Like...how does a rally about police brutality and community visibility end up being some crazy—"

"Some crazy homophobic rant!"

"Not homophobic," Toya said, shaking her head. "It's anti-gay, anti-queer, anti-...I don't know, but it ain't homophobia."

Toya's father, in response to her claim that he was a homophobic tyrant, assured her that he was in no way afraid of homosexuals. Disgusted? Yes. Disappointed and appalled? Yes. But never, ever afraid. He made that clear. So she had made it clear. If that was the way he felt, he didn't have to worry about her any more. Didn't have to be disgusted, disappointed, or appalled. "People like him ain't scared, they're ignorant and close-minded. They're—"

Nina put her finger across Toya's lips. "You know what? I don't want to talk about it anymore. Not talking about it is the essence of 'fucking it' right?" She smiled.

Toya whispered against Nina's finger. "You started it."

Nina laughed. "Well, I'm gonna finish it." She stood up slowly. She walked over to the hot tub. She reached down and flipped a gray cover up from the stone deck surrounding the Jacuzzi area. She twisted a knob in the ground and the hot tub came to life. The quiet of the night gave way to a building gurgle, the water lit up in alternating purple, green, yellow, red, and blue from the bottom. She straightened up and put her hands on her hips.

"Fuck it," Nina said again. She pulled her tank top off and stood topless. Her breasts, small and pointed, jiggled as she shimmied out of her zebra print stretch pants. No panties. She stretched up toward the sky and threw her head back before looking at Toya with invitation. "Join me," she said, turning and stepping carefully into the hot tub.

Toya watched her. She sipped her drink and watched Nina as she slid back and forth across the Jacuzzi. Night crept closer, deep blue-black spreading across the sky like spilled ink. Steam from the hot, bubbling water obscured Nina's face, but she knew she was looking at her, too. Toya took a deep breath. It seemed inappropriate. Wrong.

A day set for community building, for protest and visibility, for speaking out, hijacked by emotion and ego, arguments and idiocy. Toya went back to the moment and imagined herself punching Supreme Self in the face. She imagined grabbing

Folami by her shoulders and pressing her to take a real stand. "Say something!" she wanted to scream at her.

Toya wondered, in that moment, the first few stars of the night blazing into view, the yellow moon rising from the Bay's horizon, what Folami was doing. Was she still talking with people from the community? Was she talking with Supreme Self, Kanaan, and Fishbone? Was she challenging the ridiculous and unfounded homosexual agenda? Was she defending herself, defending her, defending their love? Or was she silent?

"Stop thinking," Nina said. "You'll ruin the moment."

Toya chuckled at Nina's word choice. Ruin. "Fuck it." She drained the last of her drink and set it down at her feet. She pushed herself up and walked toward Nina. She unbuttoned her shirt and pushed it off her shoulders. She pulled her tank top over her head, unbuckled her belt, and unfastened her shorts.

She reached the edge of the hot tub, her hands holding her shorts at her waist. Nina looked up at her, her eyes traveling from Toya's face to her breasts and stopping at her hands. Nina's lips parted. Toya smiled and let go of her shorts. They slid down her legs. She stepped out of them and eased into the water.

Toya exhaled, dipping deeper into the water. She stared up at the sky. Night had officially arrived though the moon was not yet overhead. She waved her arms back and forth in the kneading, teasing bubbles.

"Feels good, right?" Nina said. She leaned against the wall of the tub. Her skin glowed red then purple then blue as she rolled her body against the water.

"Yeah," Toya said with a sigh. "I had almost forgotten."

"Forgotten what?"

"How good Jacuzzis feel," Toya said. "I haven't been in one since…my last visit home."

"Where's home?"

"Milwaukee," Toya said. "My parents are still there. Still safe and sound in their Lake Shore mansion, view of the lake, hot tubs…" She gestured toward the house. "Very much like this place." Toya closed her eyes and saw her parents' faces, her father's scowl and her mother's frown. The lines of disappointment crinkling their eyes and drawing down their mouths.

"I don't want to talk about them though. I don't want to talk about anything," Toya said. She opened her eyes and stared up at the sky. Orion's Belt. The hunter.

Nina slid closer to her. "I don't want to talk about anything either. I don't want to talk at all," she said.

Toya brought her hand up from her lap and caressed the side of Nina's face, rubbing her full lips with an already water-wrinkled thumb. "So let's stop talking," Toya said.

Nina threw her leg over Toya's lap and straddled her. She pressed herself against Toya's stomach. Hot. Her body. The water. Everything. Hot.

Nina leaned forward and kissed Toya on the mouth. Toya kissed her back and slid her tongue into Nina's mouth as everything flushed hotter still. Toya slipped her hand beneath the water and between Nina's legs. She found her aching, arching, accepting. They pressed their mouths against each other's throats and shoulders, their tongues and lips and teeth and fingers leaving nothing unexplored. They throbbed like stars, hot, explosive. Toya let herself catapult into space, into nothingness.

BOOK V

Chapter Twenty-one

The lines blurred. Community work shouldn't be this difficult. Spending the night with Nina had been nice, and Toya hadn't felt so at ease in a long while, but even with the peace and creativity Nina provided, Toya couldn't stop thinking about Folami. And she couldn't stop thinking about the work. She went to the warehouse, where she knew Folami would be getting things prepared for the monthly community open pantry.

When Toya arrived, the side door was open. The hopper windows were closed and the industrial fan was on, but the warehouse seemed empty. She walked in and looked around. None of the food had been sorted; the empty boxes handed out to the families who came for food stood stacked against the back wall near the storage room. The long tables used to set up the outdoor pantry leaned, still folded, against the wall near the steel roll-up door.

"Folami?" Toya called out. The warehouse echoed. "Anybody here?" Toya walked toward the back storage room.

"Peace, sis," Fishbone said. "I ain't hear you come in." He nodded at Toya and hoisted a crate of apples onto his bony shoulder. A woman came out of the storage room after him, a short, light-skinned woman with red box braids and purple lipstick. She picked up a small stack of the empty boxes and wriggled her freckled nose against the dust in the air.

"Red, that's Toya," Fishbone said as he walked toward the roll-up door. "Toya, that's Red."

Toya smiled at Red and lifted her hand to wave.

"Hey," she said, hurrying over to Fishbone with the boxes clutched against her chest. He pointed at the long tables and smacked her round behind playfully before coming back over to Toya.

"Yo' girl ain't here," Fishbone said with a smirk.

"My girl?" Toya said, raising an eyebrow.

"Come on, Toya," Fishbone said. "I ain't stupid." He grabbed a bunch of his dreads in each hand and tied them into a knot at the back of his head. A few of the shorter, thicker ones sprang out. With his gaunt face and slender body, he looked like a royal palm tree.

"I know," Toya said. She looked him in his eyes but didn't say anything more.

"Hey, I don't care what y'all do. I just care about this work, ya heard me?" He shrugged. "You always been cool with me. And you know I'm down for Folami like four flat tires since way back."

"Thank you, Fish," Toya said. "Not that it matters anymore anyway."

"What you mean?" He dipped into the storage room to get another crate of apples. Toya followed him inside and made herself useful. She put her camera on a stack of wooden crates outside the storage room then grabbed two bags of potatoes.

"After the visibility event yesterday, I just don't think Folami and I are on the same page. That Supreme Self dude..." Toya stopped. She watched Fishbone's reaction to mentioning the event and the "keynote speaker." Fishbone rolled his eyes and laughed.

"I know what you talkin' about. I get it. But you know a lot of these cats be on that shit. You can't let it bother you."

"But it did, Fish. And it does." They walked the food over to the door. Red had set up two tables and worked on a third. Toya put the bags of potatoes on the second table. "It didn't seem to bother Folami at all," Toya said.

"How you know it didn't bother her?" Fishbone crossed his arms after setting the box of apples on the first table. His tattoos, barely visible against his skin, dark and smooth as Ceylon ebony, told a story. "Barbara Ann," his mother's name, ran lengthwise along his left forearm, "Never Forgotten" along his right, branded his love for a mother who died too young and too suddenly of a drug overdose. The elegant script, curls, and swirls, gave her name the elegance and dignity that abandoned her in life. A pyramid on the top of one hand, the Eye of Horus on one shoulder, and an ankh on the other, off-center and fading from his time in Coleman, spoke of books read and identities sought, the markings of a man making himself in the image of himself.

"Because..." Toya sighed. She had been in such a hurry to leave she had no idea how the discussion on the corner ended. Was that why Folami wasn't at the warehouse? Had things ended badly? Had she gotten upset and said "fuck it" in her own way?

"You don't know," Fishbone said. "You see she ain't here." He shrugged and helped Red set up the last table.

"Good point," Toya said.

"Truth be told, I ain't expect to see you here either," he said. He and Red set the table upright. He adjusted his dreads, a few of them coming loose in his efforts with the table. Red came up beside him and tucked a few errant ones inside the big knot best she could.

"People will be coming soon," Red said, her voice softer than Toya imagined, a stark contrast to her blaring red hair and assertive purple lips. Her hand lingered down Fishbone's shoulder and down his tattooed arm before she walked away.

Fishbone smiled at her backside. He shot a glance at Toya and gestured with his eyes for her approval. Toya considered Red's ass, round, high, and tight on her short frame. She nodded in appreciation. Fishbone winked at her then turned to follow Red.

"You here so you might as well help," he yelled over his shoulder as he joined Red at the first table. They adjusted the empty boxes for people to pick up, and Toya went back to the storage room to get more bags of potatoes.

❖

The few men and women who had showed up at the start of the open pantry grew to a line that wrapped around the side of the building in the first hour. They handed out potatoes, apples, carrots, wheat bread, and peanut butter. At the last table, they had stacked the canned goods—string beans, black beans, and corn. People loaded up their boxes, and when the supply waned, Fishbone and Toya went to the storage room to get more food. Each month, RiseUP! gave out food to the families in the area, giving and giving until the shelves were empty and every box full, and it was Toya's pleasure to be a part of the effort. She chatted with mothers and fathers, families and single people, trying her best to take the sting of desperation out of the charity, to expel the shadow from the brightness that was people coming together to help people.

The line moved quickly, slowing down when an elder wanted to chat about her grandchildren or the weather, the job she used to have or the recipe she had in mind for the corn. "Fried with green bell peppers and garlic, that's the way it's done," she said. Toya smiled as her grandson, a teenage boy she recognized from the corner store at the visibility event, hefted the box of food against his chest. He looked down at the box and didn't meet Toya's eyes.

The line thinned out, the canned goods nearly gone but plenty of potatoes left. Toya moved everything down from the table, then started to fold the last table when she noticed Folami

A RETURN TO ARMS

standing by the side door of the warehouse. She leaned against the wall, her arms behind her back and her legs crossed at the ankle. Her yellow denim skirt stopped short of her knees and her off-the-shoulder shirt, a men's white tee cut up and tie-dyed with red, black, and green, hung loose against her braless breasts. Her face, serious and unsmiling, shown with a soft sheen of sweat and her wild, auburn hair was snatched up into an afro puff near the top of her head, her eyes pulled tight, lips pouty and luscious in a nude gloss.

Toya swallowed hard. Why did she have to be so damn beautiful? She watched Toya close the table. Toya picked it up and used her hip to carry it over to where Folami stood. She didn't move when Toya leaned the table against the wall. She didn't speak when Toya stopped right in front of her. They stared at each other.

Toya shook her head; suddenly all the things she wanted to say, the things she rehearsed while walking from Taylor's house to the warehouse, a long walk up Eighteenth Avenue that gave her time to think, abandoned her.

"Surprised to see you here," Folami said. Her voice accusatory in a way that instantly irritated Toya.

"Don't I show up every month?" Toya said. She didn't want Folami to know that she had come to see her. She seemed smug in a way that didn't deserve her honesty.

Folami nodded. "The way you stormed off after your new friend, I figured you were done with us."

Toya scrunched her face. "Us?" Her choice of words ignited Toya's frustration. The double-talk, the double-meanings, the lack of clarity about what "us" meant from one moment to the next. Toya walked over to her.

"You don't get to just use that word like that." Toya leaned her outstretched arm against the wall, using her body to block their conversation from the last of the food line.

"Yesterday showed me that there ain't no 'us' in this thing. It's me," Toya said, pointing at her chest. "Then there's you...and them. You're with them. You're always going to be with them." Toya took a deep breath then looked Folami in the eyes. "And being with them is why you can't...why you won't be with me." Toya kept her voice low and glanced over her shoulder. Fishbone and Red stacked the empty boxes and folded the tables. A few people lingered outside the roll-up door, chatting and smiling in the late afternoon sun.

"You're making this about that?" Folami said. She pushed herself off the wall. "I knew it. I knew it would be a mistake. I knew you wouldn't be able to handle it." She rolled her eyes and sighed.

"Handle it?" Toya said. "Handle what? Standing by as you clap like a damned hypocrite? And you talking about a mistake? I cut us off!" she said. "We were done, but *you* came to my house. *You* climbed into my bed! *You* woke me up with your hands in my pants!" Toya struggled to whisper.

Fishbone cleared his throat. Folami and Toya looked over at him and Red as they pulled the warehouse door closed; Fishbone stretched up to grip the handles, and when he got it down low enough, Red helped lower it to the floor.

Folami's face flushed with embarrassment. "Come on," she said. She walked hard and fast toward the back of the warehouse. She stopped at the storage room and stood in the doorway. "Come on!" she said, putting her hands on her hips.

Toya looked over at Fishbone and Red. They both looked away, pretending it took two of them to carry one table. Toya squared her jaw and walked to the storage room. She held her hand out for Folami to go inside, then she followed. She pulled the door closed.

"I ain't trying to make a scene, but I'm disappointed in you, and I'm upset about how things went down yesterday. Even if we weren't fucking, you're my friend, Folami. Above all else, you're supposed to be my friend. That shit yesterday was foul. Beyond foul. And you ain't say shit. That's why I walked off. That's why I left."

"That's why you didn't go home?" Folami leaned against the wooden counter and drummed her nails against the edge.

"What?"

"You didn't go home." Folami's nose flared as she bit at her lower lip.

"No, I didn't," Toya said.

"And you ain't been home," she said. She gestured down at Toya's clothes, the same clothes she had worn the day before. "When you walked off, I gathered up the bag of flags you left and walked to the car. I tried to find you, but didn't know which way you went. I went to your apartment and waited. I waited a while."

"For what?" Toya shrugged. "The moment had fucking passed. There wasn't anything you could have said to me that you couldn't have said when Supreme Self stepped to us—excuse me—stepped to me with that bullshit."

"Would you just stop?" Folami said.

"Stop what, Folami?" Toya said. "Being so honest?"

"No," she said. "Being so fucking bitter."

"Bitter?!" Toya shook her head and walked toward the door.

"Yeah, bitter. You're hurt. I know I hurt you yesterday. I wanted to apologize. I waited at your place for you to show up. I didn't think you'd be here."

"Why wouldn't I be?" Toya looked at Folami over her shoulder. "It's not the community's fault you're a confused asshole."

"I'm not confused."

Toya sighed and pulled at the doorknob.

"I'm scared," Folami said.

Toya stopped. She closed the door and faced her. "Scared of what?"

"Losing what we're working so hard to build!" Her voice cracked. She swallowed and blinked her eyes rapidly, obviously fighting tears. "Did you see the momentum we had yesterday? Did you feel the energy of the crowd? Hear their voices? See their faces as they waved flags and signs?" Folami stood up straight, clutching her chest dramatically. Her wet eyes glazed over with memory. "There was power in the movement yesterday, Toya. That power is bigger than me, bigger than you, bigger than us!" She gestured at the space between them then reached out to grab Toya's arm, her hand firm and warm. "Don't you understand? I didn't agree with everything that was said on that stage. Shit, I didn't agree with most of it. But I do know that there was something moving in that place. I felt it. And when I looked around at my people lifting their fists and calling for justice, calling for change and claiming their power, I knew I was in the right place at the right time, doing the right thing. Regardless of that ignorant ass on the stage. The truth is, Toya, I care about the movement more than I care about myself. I care about my people's progress more than I care about my personal happiness."

"But what kind of life is that?"

"It's a sacrifice," Folami said. "A necessary sacrifice." She looked at Toya then, her eyes burning into her, her very soul laid bare. Serious, certain, and emboldened, she gripped Toya's arm.

"That's a sacrifice that doesn't make sense to me," Toya said. She pulled her arm away. "And it's not a sacrifice that I'm willing to make. I can't deny who I am or stand with people who think I am a tool of the enemy." Toya moved to the door and pulled it open.

"Toya," Folami said.

Toya didn't turn around. She walked through the door and picked up her camera from the tower of crates against the wall. She put the camera around her neck and made her way to the side door. Fishbone and Red sat on two crates near the roll-up door, playing with each other's fingers.

"You out?" Fishbone said, looking up and flipping a dread out of his face.

"Yeah," Toya said. She looked over her shoulder at Folami, who stood outside the storage room, her hands on her hips and eyes beckoning Toya to come back. But for what? Fishbone and Red looked from Toya to Folami and back again.

"Aight then," Fishbone said. He smiled a small smile that read like an apology.

Toya nodded and slid the locks on the side door, but before she could open it, four loud pops rang out. Loud, quick bursts that made her jump and made Red gasp. Fishbone, Red, Folami, and Toya exchanged glances as if looking to one another to confirm what they heard. Toya pulled the door open slowly.

Pop! Pop!

Toya slammed the door closed.

"Gunshots," Fishbone said.

No one moved.

CHAPTER TWENTY-TWO

Confusion. People running toward Sixteenth Street. People running from Sixteenth Street. People stood on corners and porches, crouched behind trees and parked cars. Some looked around with fear and curiosity while others hid their faces with their hands. Music blared from cars, the trembling bass and rattling treble competing with the screaming and yelling cutting through the stale, humid air.

Folami, Fishbone, Red, and Toya stood just outside the warehouse. Their heads on a swivel, watching all the activity and trying to figure out what was happening, who was shooting and why, they slowly walked into the street.

"Look!" Folami yelled and pointed toward the corner of Sixteenth Street and Eighteenth Avenue. They couldn't see for the crowd. Flashing blue and red lights made an angry disco of the intersection where men and women, all from the neighborhood, all angry and yelling, threw bottles and rocks, plastic cups and trash over their heads to the pulsing lights at the core of them.

Screaming voices asked "What are you doing?" and "Why did you shoot?" while roars of "Fuck you!" and "Put your guns down!" nearly drowned out the wailing police sirens.

Fishbone and Toya ran ahead, getting closer to see if they could ask questions about what happened. Red and Folami put their arms around each other, tears already streaming down their cheeks as they picked up their pace to catch up.

The usual scene on Sixteenth Street was laid-back, jovial even. On the weekends, as the sun set, gaggles of girls walked up and down the street, stopping to bounce a little bit to the snare and 808 of the passing Caprice classics and big body Benzes. The cars, a steady, slow-rolling parade of tropical colors and big, shimmering wheels, paused in time with beat drops to let the sun bounce off chrome grills and door handles, windows tinted but halfway down to tease the onlookers with flashes of Gucci interiors and custom steering wheels. Young boys on bikes pointed and nodded, calling out to big brothers and cousins, the grown men seated, leaning and low, a smirk of pride undeniable behind their oversized sunglasses and stiff-brimmed snapbacks.

This was not that.

People ran around screaming and crying. The crack and burst of glass bottles rivaled the blaring sirens of quickly approaching squad cars and paddy wagons. Folami caught up to Toya and Fishbone. Red stood beside a woman who held a baby on her hip, shielding the child's eyes from the fire, screams, and violence taking over the streets.

"What the fuck's going on?" Folami asked.

"I don't know!" Toya said.

Fishbone ran up to a couple of adolescent boys in Nike T-shirts and shorts who were climbing on top of a car.

"Hey, lil' homies! What's going on? What happened?" Fishbone said. He waved his arms to get the young boys' attention.

"The cops is shooting people!" one of the boys said while jockeying for position on the roof of the car.

Folami and Toya looked at each other, eyes wide and frantic. They ran toward the corner, trying to get closer to the intersection, but there were too many bodies, hot, thrashing bodies throwing bottles and rocks, shoving through each other and pumping fists.

The noise—blaring music, wailing sirens, screaming and yelling—bucked against the heat of the evening, the sky getting darker and the blue and red lights flashing. Then fire. Flames spit up from garbage cans and a loud boom made Folami, Toya, and Fishbone cower with their heads covered. Everyone around them followed suit.

Police barked orders through bullhorns and microphones attached to the tops of their vans. Their demands for people to "MOVE! MOVE! MOVE!" and "GET THE FUCK BACK! GO HOME! GO THE FUCK HOME!" were met with boos and hisses, chanting and crying. Smoke rose from the center of the crowd as police in gas masks and body shields pushed their way through the crowd.

Folami grabbed Toya's arm and pulled her out of the way as two teenagers hoisted a garbage can over their heads and threw it at a squad car that had just pulled up. The unmistakable whip and chop of a helicopter, then another. Toya and Folami looked up. A news helicopter hovered, then a police chopper with bright lights beaming down. The lights cut through plumes of smoke and gas. Fishbone came over to Folami and Toya. Red folded herself in the crook of his arm, guarding her face. Fishbone hacked and wiped his eyes.

"They got gas or pepper spray or something over there," Fishbone said, hacking. Red coughed too, her eyes red and watering.

"Anybody tell you what was going on?" Toya asked. She slipped her arm through her camera strap, wearing it across her body so she could protect it with her arm.

Fishbone and Red shook their heads.

The police helicopter, right overhead, scanned the area, and in a flash of blue-white light, Toya made out the men who had come to see Kanaan the day of the Miles Rally. They had red bandanas over their faces and they huddled together near the open trunk of a blue and gray Oldsmobile. Toya watched as one of the men pulled out a gun, a clip hanging from the middle of the gun, right in front of the handle, the barrel of the gun fashioned with small holes.

The shots flared from the gun, rapid-fire flashes of blue, red, yellow, and white. The man sprayed into the air, and the helicopter spun wildly, tiny bursts of light as bullets ricocheted off the body and tail of the chopper. The helicopter lifted and veered east. The men raised their guns and shot into the air. The cracks and pops echoing against the sirens and screams.

Chapter Twenty-three

Toya, Folami, Fishbone, and Red ran to the RiseUP! Center. The madness of the night had yet to settle. The police cars kept coming, their sirens and flashing lights as sight and sound targets for the anger of the community. The neighborhood on fire, people smashed windows and tore down signs of local businesses. The convenience store bum-rushed by young men with broom handles and bats; Badcock Furniture, the first store of its kind to extend credit to Black customers, suffered bricks through showcase windows and sofas set ablaze.

"It's crazy out there," Folami said once they made it inside. Out of breath and sweaty, Toya and Folami collapsed on the couch while Red, who wouldn't leave Fishbone's side, continued to rub at her eyes in between hacking coughs.

"We know," Kanaan said. He stood in the middle of the living room with his arms folded across his chest. He wore a white tank top and camouflage pants. His gun stuck out the front of his pants, the handle resting on the edge of his thick black belt. Behind him, at the dining room table, sat Supreme Self, the short announcer-phlegm man, and two men Toya didn't recognize.

"Where's Director Abasi?" Fishbone asked.

"He's supposedly on his way," Kanaan said. "I wouldn't be surprised if he was scared to leave his house." He chuckled and Supreme Self laughed through his teeth. A serpent like hiss that made him seem all the more lizard-like when he licked his lips and leaned back in his chair.

"Do you know what happened?" Toya said. She sat up on the sofa, adjusting her camera strap and setting the camera against her stomach. She slid her hand across her slick forehead then wiped the sweat on her pants.

Kanaan looked over his shoulder as if trying to decide if he should say anything. Supreme Self nodded and shrugged.

"Young brother got pulled over by the pigs. Young brother got killed by the pigs," Kanaan said.

"Pig unloaded his whole clip. Right into the windshield. Blam! Blam! Blam! Like a Black life ain't shit." One of the men seated near Supreme Self pushed himself away from the table. He continued. "I was right there. Saw the whole thing. Pulled my man over right at the intersection of Eighteenth and Sixteenth. Before we knew it, shots." He held his arms out in front of him, his hands holding an imaginary gun. "Blam! Blam! Blam!" he said again, pointing his fake gun right at Toya.

Toya swallowed and sat back slowly. Hot tears assaulted the rims of her eyes. She took a deep breath and tried to blink them away. It didn't work. Folami sat up, her eyes wet with tears, too.

Kanaan shook his head. "Save your tears," he said.

Supreme Self stood up. "The time for crying is over, Queens. It's time for action."

Folami put her hand on Toya's knee and pushed herself up from the couch. She looked over at Fishbone and Red, then glanced back at Toya. She wiped her eyes.

"What y'all gonna do?" Folami said.

Kanaan smirked. "We setting up this weekend. Right at the scene of the murder."

Fishbone eased himself from Red's grip. "You know it's gonna be curfews and shit in effect after tonight's get down," he said. Red grabbed his hand; he brought it to his mouth and kissed it before holding it at his side.

"Of course," Supreme Self said. "I don't give a fuck about no faggot ass curfew. Do you?" He grinned and looked at Folami and Toya before raising his eyebrow at Fishbone.

"We got some planning to do," Kanaan said. "Who's in?"

Fishbone shrugged and pulled Red along with him into the dining room. Supreme Self sat in his original seat as Kanaan stared Folami and Toya down.

Toya stood up. "I'm out." She looked over at Folami, who refused to return her gaze. Folami took a deep breath that she didn't exhale until she took a seat in the dining room across from Supreme Self. Kanaan laughed. Toya left.

❖

Toya arrived at the creamy pink and white mansion physically exhausted but spirited in heart and mind. It had been difficult to get a cab, but once she got one and directed it around all the smoke and fire that had consumed the better part of Midtown, the ride had been a welcome moment of silent reflection and strategic planning. The cab driver, a plum-colored man with kind eyes and brilliantly white teeth, said he was praying for the people of America before he turned up the volume dial on the stereo. A slow song played, bongos and woodwinds dancing a waltz with a woman's haunting voice. The vocalist's humming, moaning, rolling baritone cleared Toya's mind, smoothed the knots in her shoulders. By the time she got dropped at Taylor's house, she knew exactly what she needed to do.

"Hey," Ray said. He opened the door wide and pulled Toya inside quickly. "You okay? Me and Nina were just talking about you. We were praying, chile! It's crazy out there!"

"I'm fine," Toya said.

"You want a drink?" Ray said. He wore long, flowing yellow pants and a white V neck shirt.

Toya shook her head. She looked around the living room. A couple of men, or women, or a man and a woman, Toya couldn't tell which, held each other and snored softly on the sofa. The back patio was dark, even with the small yellow lights dotting the perimeter of the area. Taylor lay on the floor near the fireplace, his face buried in a book.

"He's reading *Kindred*," Ray said, following Toya's eyes. "And you bet not dog-ear any of my pages!" he snapped at Taylor, who waved him off without taking his eyes off the page.

"Where's Nina?" Toya asked.

"Upstairs," Ray said as he made his way to the bar. "You can go up." He waved his hand toward the winding staircase.

Toya rubbed her sweaty palms on her jeans, gripped her camera under her arm with one hand, and walked up the stairs. The sweet, woodsy smell of marijuana mixed with comforting hints of freesia as Toya made her way down the dark hallway. She followed the sound of Meshell Ndegeocello's strumming bass and velvet-smooth voice, which led her to a partially closed door after an abrupt turn at the end of the hall. She knocked on the door.

Toya knocked again, nudging the door open a little with her foot. Shadows danced across the walls, candlelight flickered at the tips of pillar candles, and smoke weaved around the room.

"Come inside," Nina said, her voice husky and slow. Another voice, light and giggly, repeated her response then burst into laughter.

Toya stepped inside the room. Nina, wearing a white tank top and turquoise and white striped boy shorts, waved Toya inside with a seductive smile. She lounged across a collection of oversized pillows of assorted colors. Nearby, a white woman, wearing royal blue stretch pants and a red Super Mario Brothers T-shirt, crawled into the center of a red hang-a-round chair with gleaming silver legs. She smiled too, her icy blue eyes and raven black hair contrasting the friendliness of her grin. She reached over to a small white lacquered table to pick up her nearly empty wine glass.

"You're safe," Nina said. She held her hand out for Toya to take it.

Toya stepped forward and took her hand. She let Nina guide her to take a seat on the pillows beside her.

"So you heard about the riots?" Toya said.

"Who hasn't?" the white woman said. She sipped her wine. "Is it as bad as it looks on the news?

Nina shot her a look. "It never is, Sophie," she said. She returned her attention to Toya. "Were you in it?"

Toya nodded. "On the fringes. We couldn't get too close because of the crowds. There were a lot of people out there. We left before it got too bad."

Nina frowned with concern then placed her hand on Toya's hand. "I'm just glad you're okay. And I'm glad you came here." She smiled again and ran her fingers across Toya's knuckles.

"I didn't know where else to go," Toya said. She glanced over at Sophie then back at Nina. "I need to talk to you."

Nina nodded. "Sophie, why don't you go hang out downstairs for a while? Your crisis is over, right? Go relax. Be social. Have fun." She waved her hand at Sophie as she stood up and walked toward the door with her empty wine glass.

"Fine," Sophie said with a shrug. "You're out of wine anyway." She left the room, leaving the door wide open.

Nina pushed herself up and walked over to close the door. "Sophie is going through a breakup. She's been talking my ear off for over an hour." She rolled her eyes and sat on the pillows next to Toya. "All this shit going on, and she talking about unreturned text messages."

Toya shifted on the pillows. She bit her lip and tried to think of the best way to begin. She had a plan in mind for a response to the shooting, but she couldn't do it alone. Folami had made her choice, and that choice left Toya feeling alone but determined. "I've never seen a riot with my own eyes. Pictures. Videos. But nothing like being there. Seeing it. Smelling it. Hearing it."

"How bad was it?" Nina asked.

"Angry. Loud. Sad." Toya stared down at her feet. "Stores and cars on fire. Tear gas. Smoke." Tears welled in Toya's eyes. "Children. There were kids out there. Families. How does an evening hangout become a riot? How does everything get so out of hand?" She couldn't hold the tears back. She cried, her shoulders shaking and chin trembling. Nina put her arm around her and pulled her close.

"I know. I know," Nina whispered against the top of Toya's head. Her lips pressed through Toya's small afro.

"They killed another one. The police killed another one. On the spot. He didn't even get a chance to get out of the car," Toya said, choking on sobs. "And what do they expect? We're just supposed to do nothing? We just do nothing?" She buried her face into Nina's small breasts and let the tears come as Nina rocked her and rubbed her back.

"I'm sorry," Toya said. She swallowed hard and took a deep breath in an effort to stop crying. She slowly lifted her head and wiped her face with the back of her hand.

"You don't have to apologize," Nina said. "You had to get it out."

Toya pressed her fingers into her eyelids as if squeezing out the last of her tears. She exhaled loudly.

"Where's Folami? Why aren't you with her?" Nina said.

Toya shook her head. "She's with...we're not working together anymore."

Nina nodded. "I see." She stretched her strong but petite legs out in front of her.

"It doesn't matter anyway," Toya said. "I've got a plan. And if you'll help me, I won't need her."

"Okay," Nina said. "What do you have in mind?"

"A demonstration. A march from the scene of the shooting to downtown St. Pete. Williams Park." Toya's eyes widened with excitement.

"Downtown?" Nina raised an eyebrow.

"Yeah. Downtown. And it's got to happen soon. Like in the next day or two."

"Let's do it. I'm in. Whatever you need," Nina said. "Anything at all."

Toya took a deep breath. "I'm going to need a lot of help. I've got posters and flyers to make, images to print, and videos to edit. I need gallons of red paint and a way to hook up a projector for mobile use. I need a wagon and a portable screen. I need people to canvas with flyers, every neighborhood in this city. I need people. Lots and lots of people." Her chest heaved with excitement.

"Is this going to be possible?"

Nina reached behind her to snatch a thin, smoking cigar out of a black and white ashtray shaped like a hand. She took a long pull then blew the smoke over her head. "Anything is possible."

Chapter Twenty-four

The copy shop filled quickly, faster than Toya imagined it would. The swoosh and click of copy machines accompanied the excited snatches of in-depth conversation and animated introductions of the varied collections of people who made their way into the meeting. Mr. Aaron had agreed to open the store two hours early and do the event copying for free. He and Thelonius jumped at the chance to help once Toya explained her plans.

"My wife," Mr. Aaron had said, his eyes tearing up and his bald head dipping down to hide them, "My wife would have been front and center. She would have been right on the front lines. And we would have been with her." He had taken a deep breath and smoothed the front of his short-sleeved dress shirt. "So we'll be right with you." Toya had thanked him and gave him the files for copying. Thelonius put on Coltrane's *Love Supreme* and started the jobs—flyers, posters, and banners with "Black Lives Matter," "No Justice, No Peace," and "Stop Police Brutality" printed on them. There were one-page information sheets with the profiles of recent and past cases of police using deadly force on unarmed citizens and a single-spaced document that listed names, just the names, of men and women killed by police in the past year.

"There were this many?" Thelonius said as he loaded the print job. "Just last year?"

"Yeah," Toya said. "It's something when you see them all listed like that ain't it?"

Nina clapped her hands and called the meeting to order. She looked over all the attendees and glanced over at Toya before she began. Toya nodded.

"We're so glad you all came this morning. I know it's short notice, but then again, justice been long overdue!" Nina said. Hands clapped and a few people shouted out "Right on!" and "You right!"

"There's a big job in front of us. We're attempting to do something the likes of St. Petersburg has never seen. We're going to shut this city down! We're going to make this city feel our pain and hear our voices!" Nina pumped her fist and moved aside for Toya to come forward.

Toya looked out at the people who filled the shop. A few faces she recognized from RiseUP! meetings were there, a petite woman with sandy brown dreads down to her waist and a long T-shirt with the words "Mama Africa" across the front stood with five other light-skinned women, dreads and afros of varying lengths and sizes, African jewelry accenting their denim skirts and political sloganed T-shirts. A family, each member the same shade of russet brown with the same broad, friendly smiles, took up a corner near the self-serve copiers. The college students from the pre-rally meeting were there, too, with at least a dozen of their friends. A multi-cultural group, the students wore T-shirts and hats boasting Black Student Union, LGBTQ-Action, and Latino Student Association membership. Along with the familiar faces were not-so-familiar faces. A group of older white women with short, silver hair, lots of bracelets, and dangly earrings stood near the counter. They wore running shoes with their flowing skirts and loose-fitting tunics. There was a small network of Bohemian-looking women, long chestnut brown hair and thrift store sundresses, flowers behind their ears, and patchwork satchels. They leaned against tall, lanky white boys with cropped hair, hemp necklaces, and skinny jeans.

Toya cleared her throat, suddenly nervous with so many strangers looking at her, and looking *to* her for leadership. She closed her eyes, and scenes from the rally flashed across the inside of her eyelids. The people, the music. She heard the choir rising up in the back of her mind, the chanting for blood, and then sirens, rapid gunfire. She opened her eyes. She opened her mouth.

"BLACK LIVES MATTER!" she roared. The room held still.

"That's why I'm here," Toya said. "And I hope that's why you're here." She took a deep breath. "I'm surprised to see so many of you. Pleasantly surprised, but so very thankful. I've been having a difficult time this past year especially, trying to make sense of what looks and sounds and feels like the systematic murder of people who look like me. It's been frustrating because we ain't talking about Black crime, and we ain't talking about murder in general." She gestured to Thelonius and Nina to hand out the one-page printouts of the names. "This is a list of all the UNARMED Black women, men, and CHILDREN who have been murdered by police in the last year. Many of these murders went under-reported. Many of them resulted in nothing more than an officer being suspended with pay—"

"Just like the officers in the Lewis shooting right here!" the petite woman with the long dreads said, her voice bigger than Toya expected. "Suspended *with* pay!" People shook their heads and mumbled curses under their breath.

"Exactly," Toya said. "This isn't a coincidence. These cases are not isolated incidents. They are all connected. They are all symptoms of a centuries old problem, a cancer that continues to rot our country to the core."

"Racism!" a short white woman yelled from near the front counter. People clapped and nodded.

"Look, I don't know how Nina got so many of y'all to come out. And I am thankful for the people here who I know…" Toya smiled at the women from RiseUP! "...who decided to join this ambitious, optimistic, and inspired march. I hate to sound cliché, but I have a good feeling about this. We gonna shut this city down. We gonna make everyone take notice. We are gonna make a difference." She went on to share the details of the march, which would take them two-and-a-half miles from the scene of the shooting to Williams Park in downtown St. Pete. She outlined the canvassing they'd do the rest of the day, sharing information about the march and about the cases at hand.

The reactions were enthusiastic; people talked among themselves about what parts of town they would go to and made plans to meet up in Midtown on the launch day. Nina coordinated with Taylor and Ray, who had volunteered to take care of the projector, screen, and red paint. As the conversation hit a fever pitch, Toya raised a hand to get people's attention. It didn't work.

Toya climbed up on the counter. "BLACK LIVES MATTER! BLACK LIVES MATTER!"

Everyone in the shop, from the door to the counter, from the copiers to the desktop computers, echoed Toya's cry.

"BLACK LIVES MATTER! BLACK LIVES MATTER! BLACK LIVES MATTER!"

The chanting picked up speed, rose in volume, the entire copy shop seeming to rattle with the power of their voices.

CHAPTER TWENTY-FIVE

Toya collapsed onto the sectional. Nina sat in the chair across from her, resting her bare feet on the low table between them. Taylor and Ray were still inside the house finishing up the last of the calls. They had been tasked with calling everyone in their contacts lists to come out to the march. After the pep rally of sorts at the print shop, everyone had assignments—handing out flyers about the event, calling their friends and family to recruit for the event, and coordinating rides to get people to the march's staring point, the very intersection where TyRon Lewis had been killed.

"I'm exhausted," Toya said. "And it's still so hot." She sighed and covered her face with her hands. The slight breeze coming off the bay did little to cool the humid night air.

"You want to get in the pool?" Nina said. "It might cool you off."

Toya sat up slowly and shook her head. "I should probably go home. I still have to work on the final edits to the videos." She yawned.

"You're tired. Maybe you should relax a while. Take a moment to exhale." Nina moved her feet from the table and stood up. She made her way over to where Toya sat and knelt between her legs. "I can help you relax," she said. Nina put her hands on Toya's thighs and massaged them through her jeans then stretched herself up to kiss Toya's lips.

Toya kissed her back, reluctantly at first before giving in to the warm demand of Nina's mouth. She reached up and took Nina's face in her hands as they kissed with more urgency.

Nina moaned, pressing herself more fully into the space between Toya's legs and wrapping her arms around Toya's waist. Toya tried losing herself in the stroke of Nina's tongue and the softness of her lips. She closed her eyes and hoped for calm in the darkness behind her eyelids. Instead, the black swirled with memory. A voice, faint but recognizable in the corner of her mind. The song from the rally. *I'm on my way.* Faces. Fire. Blood. Bodies. Shouting strangers and persistent police. Signs shaking in protest and voices raised in frustration.

"Wait," Toya whispered. She fought the vision. Tried to push the rally, the riot, the fainting out of her mind. "Wait, wait," she repeated in between kisses. "I can't," she said, opening her eyes.

Nina pulled back. "What? Why? What's wrong?"

"I'm just...I can't relax." She sighed.

"Is it her?" Nina said, resting back on her feet.

"No," Toya said. "No." She shook her head. "It's the work. I can't stop thinking about the work." She put her hands on Nina's shoulders and squeezed. She leaned forward and kissed Nina on the forehead.

"You know, it's okay," Nina said. She pushed herself up from the sandstone floor. She stood over Toya with her hands on her small hips.

"What's okay?' Toya looked up at her.

Nina smiled. "If you still love her. Love is a beautiful thing. It's the only thing really."

Toya smiled and nodded.

"Come on. I'll take you home." Nina turned and headed inside the house.

❖

Toya sat on the couch, her computer humming and hot on her lap. She had started editing the videos she'd shot with Folami but had to stop. It was difficult to watch her on the screen, frustrating to hear her voice. Instead, Toya worked on a slideshow using the images from the rally, the Johnston funeral, a few Internet images—portraits of the unarmed Black women, men, and children killed by police in the last year. She edited images to make them sharper, using software to crop and adjust tones, to highlight and reduce blur.

A knock on the door interrupted her work.

She placed the computer on the sofa and stood to answer the door. She looked into the peephole. Folami, her afro held back with a wide yellow headband and face pulled down into a frown, stood outside Toya's door. She opened it slowly.

"Yes," Toya said.

"Hi," Folami said.

"What do you want?"

"Can I come in?" Folami took a deep breath and looked into Toya's eyes. "I need…" She looked away and when she returned her gaze to Toya, tears filled her eyes.

Toya saw hurt in Folami's eyes. Confusion and a hint of fear. She stepped back and let Folami in. Toya went to the couch and placed the computer on the floor as she took a seat beside Folami, who had wasted no time sitting down.

"What's wrong?" Toya asked. "You're trembling. What happened?"

Folami wiped her eyes. "This evening's meeting was terrible. It was just…the people Kanaan invited and the men Supreme Self brought with him to the center tonight." She shook her head. "It started out with talk about Lewis, about the shooting and the community response. Then, the conversation took a turn. Kanaan said something about the cops being faggots, and at the mention of the word, Supreme Self took off on one of his rants."

Toya rolled her eyes and shook her head. "I told you…"

"I know," Folami said. A tear dripped down her cheek. She wiped it with her fingers then continued. "It was worse this time. So much worse. Fishbone and Red left a little after you did. There were only two other women there. Me and this pregnant woman who came with one of Supreme's friends. Kanaan joined in with Supreme. Everything was faggot this and dyke bitch that. They kept talking about how people who stood in their way had to die. That war is the only way. They were full of so much hate. The way they were going on, Toya, I just...I couldn't sit there and listen to it. I went to the bathroom and just stayed in there. I stayed in there and cried. I wanted them to stop. I wanted them to stop talking about hurting people, murdering for the cause." She cried then, the tears falling and her bottom lip trembling.

"You're safe now," Toya said. "You're safe here." She put her hand on Folami's knee.

"So, I stayed in the bathroom."

Toya nodded and squeezed Folami's knee.

"It took me a while, but I managed to stop crying." Folami stopped. "Then someone banged on the bathroom door. Hard. It scared me. I realized in that moment why I was crying. It wasn't just the negativity. I was afraid. I was in a room with men who were supposed to be my brothers, but I was scared of them, of what they might say, what they might do. To me." Folami burst into tears anew. "I was scared they would do something to me because of how I am. Who I am."

Toya took Folami in her arms and held her tighter than she'd ever held anyone in her life. Folami's body shuddered in her embrace. "It's okay," Toya said. "You're safe. You're safe."

Folami finally wrapped her arms around Toya and they held each other in silence. As Folami's tears lessened and her breathing slowed to something almost normal, Toya began rubbing Folami's back in small circles. She whispered into Folami's ear.

"The day of the Miles rally," she began, "I fainted. The music, the chanting, all the people, I don't know what it was, but it did something to me. I felt…something in me…my spirit moved." She licked her lips, her tongue inadvertently grazing Folami's ear. "While I was down, passed out, unconscious or whatever, I saw…I heard…I don't know how to explain it. Not quite a vision but not really a memory either. I don't know. It still confuses me. But the feeling. The feeling, Folami, was real. What I feel, everything I feel, is real. And important."

Folami slowly eased her face from the crook of Toya's neck, which was sticky-hot with sweat and tears. Toya put a little space between them but didn't break their embrace.

"You fell out? Why didn't you tell me?" Folami said. Her eyes swollen and red from her crying, her forehead wrinkled with concern.

"I didn't know how. I didn't know what you'd say." Toya shrugged. "If you'd think it was stupid. If you'd dismiss it like… like you've dismissed everything else I've felt."

Folami shook her head. "I am so sorry. I am so very sorry." She pulled her arms from Toya's waist and wiped her eyes with the backs of her hands. "I've been so stupid. I've been stupid and…afraid. It's fear. Just like tonight when I locked myself in that bathroom. I've been scared of the only thing that has made me feel safe." She nodded and swallowed hard. "This." She gestured at the space between them. "Us. This is where I'm safe. Always." She blinked, and one more tear, a final tear, made its way down her cheek. Toya wiped it, and Folami leaned forward. Toya held Folami's face and looked into her eyes.

"I love you," Folami said. "And I'm not afraid anymore."

Chapter Twenty-six

Toya woke with a start from a dreamless sleep. The sun had yet to clear the houses and buildings, so the room was washed in a gentle but persistent blue. Toya glanced over at Folami, who snored softly beside her in bed. They had stayed up late. Toya filled Folami in on the idea for the march, told her about the meeting at the copy shop, and how she had been recruiting lots of help. Folami had loved the idea and couldn't wait to get to work. After editing the videos where Folami gave overviews of all the police brutality and controversial shootings, they had made love all night long, slow and careful, as if the love between them was new and fragile. She watched Folami, the rise and fall of her breasts beneath the sheet, the flare of her nostrils, and the rhythmic puffs of air that escaped her pouty lips. Toya leaned over and softly kissed the still sweat-damp hair at her temple. She crept out of bed and searched for her pants in the darkness. When she found them, she dug in the pocket for her phone.

Once in the living room, Toya stood, hands clasped around her cell phone, and stared at her poster of Fannie Lou Hamer. She'd always wished her mother had been strong like Hamer. Outspoken and unrelenting, passionate and resilient. Instead, her mother had always stood silently by as her father dictated the ways in which their small family would live and love.

Toya pressed the button to listen to her voicemails. She skipped through all the new messages, more than likely people with questions about the march later that morning. When she got to her saved messages, she held her breath.

Her mother's voice, clear but slightly timid, came through the phone, and just like the first time Toya listened to the message, she was struck by how old she sounded. Her voice gritty and low. Perhaps she had been crying. Perhaps all she did was cry. Toya exhaled the breath she was holding as she listened to the rest of the message and felt herself nearly collapse with the way the message ended. "I'm telling you all this because I'm sorry. I've made so many mistakes. And I'm sorry. I just need you to know that. Whether we ever speak again or not, I'm sorry for my silence. I'm sorry for being so weak. I love you, LaToya. I always have. I always will."

Toya looked at the phone, and with tears in her eyes, scrolled through her call history for the missed call with the Milwaukee area code. She hovered her thumb over the number and blinked against the burning in her eyes. She took a deep breath and pressed call.

The phone rang twice before Toya's mother answered.

"Hello? LaToya?" Her mother's voice seemed far away, like a dream, like the whispers that haunted Toya when she had fainted.

"Yes," Toya said. "It's me."

Her mother sobbed into the phone, and the sound of her crying split Toya's heart in two.

"My baby. I can't believe it's my baby," her mother said. "I'm so sorry, baby. I'm so very, very sorry, LaToya. Please, please forgive me." She sniffled and choked on her words, her sobs fighting with her sentences.

"I...I...I don't know if...I'll try, Mama." Toya coughed, choking too, crying too. "I'll try."

Chapter Twenty-seven

Toya and Folami arrived at the meeting place early. Across the street from the burned out convenience store, Kanaan, Fishbone, Supreme Self, and a few other people set up tables and a vinyl tent. The long Ford truck sat off to the side, Dead Presidents blaring from the speakers. Toya and Folami stood on the opposite corner with a wagon Toya borrowed from Mr. Aaron. Boxes of flyers, three bullhorns, and a duffel bag with her camera and tripod shifted inside the wagon as she pulled it closer to her.

Nina, Ray, and Taylor arrived with two more wagons. Larger and brand new, one of the red wagons held over fifty quarter-pint cans of red paint. In the other wagon, Ray had strapped a mobile wireless projector on top of a stack of books.

"Is this what you had in mind?" Ray said. He pursed his lips and winked.

"Exactly what I had in mind," Toya said.

"Um, Nina, Ray, Taylor, this is Folami," Toya said. She fixed her eyes on Nina, who smiled and winked at her.

"Hey, sis," Nina said. "I'm glad you could make it." She held out her hand.

Folami looked at Toya for a split second, and a question seemed to flash in her eyes. Toya nodded and smiled, trying to reassure her, hoping that her eyes reminded Folami of their love, their connection, their bond. Folami smiled back, a small, knowing smile, before turning to Nina.

"Hey," Folami said, opening her arms to give Nina and her friends welcoming hugs.

"Now that we all know each other," Toya said with a clap of her hands. "Where's the screen?"

Nina dug around in her denim shoulder bag and pulled out a large, folded white sheet. "Will this do?"

Toya nodded. "And sound?"

Taylor took a Bluetooth speaker out of his leather messenger bag. He held it up then nestled it between the projector and the side of the wagon. "Oh, we got this!" he said, flipping his hair out of his eyes.

"This is going to be too perfect!" Nina said.

Toya asked Folami for her phone, which they had used to upload videos to YouTube as well as backups to an online drop box. The videos Toya and Folami had shot made for compelling three-minute overviews of the cases. And the slideshows of the portraits and footage from the rally was a great addition to the overall visuals. Folami had also added large text captions of the victims' names—Oscar Grant, Tamir Rice, Rekia Boyd, Kathryn Johnston, Mike Brown, Freddie Gray, Miriam Carey, Tanisha Anderson, and Yvette Smith—and their ages. Toya brought the videos up and showed Nina how to access them so she could work with Taylor and Ray to set them up for projection and sound.

As they worked on the particulars, people began showing up for both the march and the event across the street. The corner filled as people checked in at the long table, grabbing color pamphlets and standing around the tent where Supreme Self stood behind a small podium. There was a table with T-shirts and other items on the side of the tent near the truck. Fishbone and Red sat on the extended tailgate of the truck, both of them scrolling on their phones. Kanaan walked around raising his fist as people walked up, giving a handshake to men who came his way and one-armed hug to the few women who followed close behind. Toya watched him, anger about the story Folami had told her about the last meeting burning in the center of her chest. Kanaan looked up. They stared at each other, separated by the two lanes of Eighteenth Avenue. A few cars passed between them, but no gestures or words.

Nina walked up behind Toya. "Did you know they were having an event the same day?"

Toya shook her head. "I wasn't sure. It doesn't matter though."

"Sure doesn't. We got enough to worry about over here anyway." Nina nudged her chin in the direction of a small group of people who were arriving. Nina walked away and greeted them as they crowded around the wagons with their signs and banners, flyers and posters. There were the posters with words and few posters with blown up portraits of those murdered by the police. The images, large and detailed, dramatic and compelling, would say to those looking on what words sometimes failed to say. The eyes, the smiles, the faces would say loud and clear that Yvette Smith was a person. That Tamir Rice was a child.

As more people gathered on the corner, Toya explained more about the cans of paint. She motioned for Folami to pick up a can and hold it overhead.

Toya raised her voice to get the attention of the small group of people. "I'm anticipating police interference. Based on the riots here the other night, the paid leave the murdering officers are enjoying, and the city curfew, I'm expecting riot gear." She bent over to pick up a can of paint. She had a couple of the college students pry open the tops halfway so they'd be easy to open. "Now I know it's dangerous. I'm scared, too. But I'm more enraged than scared. More angry than afraid." She made eye contact with the twenty or so people who had gathered around.

Toya lifted up a can of paint. "This paint is red. Red like blood. Like the blood of those slain. The blood of those left to die in the street, no voice to tell their side of the story, only blood screaming red. When the police come up on us, I want you to throw this paint in their faces or, if you don't feel comfortable doing that, you can pour it on yourself."

Nina picked up a can and added, "We want the police to see red. We want the onlookers to see red. We want them to understand that this thing is about blood, and at the end of the day, we all bleed red."

"Innocent Black blood spilled in the street is blood splashed on all of us, and everything we hold dear," Folami said. Toya watched as Nina and Folami shared a quick smile.

The three of them lifted the paint cans and yelled, "BLACK LIVES MATTER! BLACK LIVES MATTER!"

People hoisted their signs and flyers. They joined in the chant, a few of them stepping forward to take a can of paint out of the wagon. At the sound of the chanting, some of the people from across the street looked over at them. They walked toward the corner and nudged each other, pointing and turning to talk to Fishbone and Kanaan, more than likely asking what was going on and if the events were related. Toya shrugged off the interest from the people across the street and walked over to the wagon with her camera and the bullhorns. She handed bullhorns to Ray, Folami, and Nina, along with a sheet of names. They were to say the names repeatedly as they marched.

A silver minivan pulled up at the corner where Toya and the marchers were getting organized. The door slid open and eight teenagers climbed out of the back. An older Black gentleman with a white afro rolled down the passenger side window. "This here the march?"

Yes, sir," Toya said.

"Good," the man said. He climbed out of the van and told the driver to park nearby.

After the van, more people came, hopping out of trucks and cars, pulling up on scooters and bicycles. Across the street, people filled the tent area and overflowed to the corner. The music blasted louder as more people showed up, and once people from RiseUP! started recognizing each other, they walked back and forth across the street, comparing events and shrugging at the differences.

At ten a.m., Toya picked up her bullhorn and sounded the alarm. A high-pitched siren cut through the afternoon heat. The people gathered on the corner quieted and looked in her direction. Nina stood on her tiptoes trying to count how many people had showed up. She shook her head and frowned, starting over as people shifted, coming from across the street and leaving to cross the street and back again.

From the looks of it, Toya estimated almost a hundred people stood on the corner waiting to get started. She spoke into the bullhorn. "We're about to start. We want to stagger as much as possible. Try not to walk in groups more than three across. Follow the banner and the screen, the wagons are leading the way. Are you ready? BLACK LIVES MATTER!"

"BLACK LIVES MATTER! BLACK LIVES MATTER!"

While Toya led the chant, Nina directed Taylor and two other tall men who came to the march to take the first shift of holding the screen. They stood shoulder to shoulder, each holding the sheet along the top. They positioned themselves behind the wagon with the projector.

"The slideshow or the videos?" Nina asked.

Toya looked over at Folami, who tapped her chin in thought, then cast her vote for the slideshow to start. Nina cued up the slideshow on the phone, connected with the speaker and projector, and pushed play. Across the screen, a slideshow of faces, repeated images from the rally, and bold text of their names, block letters in bright red across the black-and-white portraits.

"You ready?" Toya asked Folami. She placed her hands on Folami's shoulders and squeezed.

"Are *you* ready?" Folami said. She smiled. Toya kissed Folami, and Folami kissed her back, in full view of everyone, a statement and sentiment, fact and feeling finally coming together in full. When they parted, a few people cheered, clapping and making silly faces. Nina gave Toya a smile and quick head nod. Ray chuckled and shook his head.

"So that's what it is?" Kanaan's voice caught Folami and Toya by surprise as it boomed from beyond a couple of college students adjusting their signs.

"That's what what is, Kanaan?" Toya said. She handed Folami her bullhorn and stepped through the students to face Kanaan head-to-head.

"I told you this shit was divisive. You might as well be working for the state pulling brothers and sisters who should be standing with us and getting them all fucked up with this sideshow." He looked around at the crowd and shook his head in disapproval.

Toya considered the collection of protestors too. Varied and eclectic, they all had one thing in common. They all believed that Black lives mattered.

"Kanaan, why don't you go back across the street?" Folami said.

Kanaan glanced at her then dismissed her with a twist of his lips. "I'm surprised at you, Folami. Or maybe I ain't. You fit right into the sideshow, too. Don't know what got your mind twisted, but…whatever." He turned his attention back to Toya, his hands on his narrow hips, his sunglasses reflecting the crowd and a burst of sunlight. "It's really too bad. You got the passion. The intellect. It's a waste. A real waste." He shook his head.

Toya looked at Kanaan. She crossed her arms and squared her shoulders. "I've been thinking the exact same thing about you."

"Fuck you," Kanaan said. When Toya didn't respond, he continued. Kanaan threw his head back with forced laughter. "Might be just the thing you need to correct yourself. Get you back to your Afrikan roots." He grabbed at the crotch of his baggy khaki pants.

"What?" Toya pushed Kanaan in the chest. He stumbled backward then caught himself. He lunged at Toya. Out of the corner of her eye, as she struggled to get Kanaan's hands off of her, Toya saw Ray ram through the people who gathered around the scuffle. Ray grabbed Kanaan by the neck of his black T-shirt and yanked him backward. Folami raised the bullhorn and came charging toward the tussling collection of hands and arms Kanaan, Ray, and Toya had become.

Folami pressed the siren button and people stopped and looked around worriedly for police before realizing it was the bullhorn and settling down. Fishbone and Red had made it over to the scuffle just as Ray reared back his fist to knock Kanaan on his ass. Fishbone pulled Kanaan away just in time. Ray toppled forward with the missed punch. Folami caught him and helped him steady himself. Toya caught her breath as Fishbone wrapped his long arms around Kanaan and practically carried him away and into the street.

"Why the fuck are you even over here!" Toya yelled to Kanaan, who gestured wildly with his hands while Fishbone tried in vain to calm him down. Toya wiped at her mouth, a little blood from a small cut smeared on the back of her hand. She glared at Kanaan. "Take your fucked up attitude and—"

Nina put a hand on Toya's arm. "He's gone," she said. "Let's let it go. Let's focus on our event. Please."

"Yeah, we don't want to draw any attention too early. We haven't even started marching," Taylor said. He flipped his bangs and looked at Toya with concern in his arctic blue eyes.

Folami moved toward Toya. She grabbed her hand and pulled her away from Nina and Taylor. She held Toya's face and wiped at the cut in Toya's lip with her thumb. "We know Kanaan is a supreme asshole. That's why him and that other supreme asshole get along so well."

Toya forced a smile. Her lip hurt.

"Fuck him. Fuck both of them." Folami kissed Toya lightly. "Look at all these people."

Toya looked over her shoulder. There were even more people than when she gave her initial instructions about paint.

"See all those people? They're here to march. They're here for the struggle." Folami grinned. "Let's march. Let's move. Forward." She pressed her lips to Toya's lips once more.

"I'm ready," Toya said, kissing Folami one last time. "Let's move."

Toya and Folami made their way to the front of the crowd. Nina handed them both bullhorns. Toya glanced over her shoulder. Kanaan and Fishbone were standing near the traffic signal across the street, still talking. The music at their event had stopped. Supreme Self had moved from the podium inside the tent to stand in the back of the truck. Instead of a bullhorn, he had a microphone and large amplifier. He started talking, a smooth appeal that in light of the shooting here at home, it was time to act.

"There is no room in this revolution for Afrikans who want to stand idly by and watch the police state and armies of faggots and white devils set up camp in their neighborhoods. You cannot stand idly by and let them destroy our families, our very futures! THIS MEANS WAR!" he yelled.

Some of the people standing in the tent and gathered around the truck clapped their hands and lifted their fists. Some did not.

"THIS MEANS WAR!" he yelled again. "WE WILL NOT STAND IDLY BY!"

Toya kissed Folami once more then grabbed her bullhorn. She glanced across the street then fixed her eyes on the people in front of her. The mix of people—youth and elder, men and women, queer and not, black and not—who stood united in front of her. All them there for the same cause; all of them there to raise their voices and move their feet for the same cause. All of them, knowing and understanding, that injustice for one is an injustice for all, and oppression is oppression is oppression.

Toya lifted the bullhorn to her mouth. "BLACK LIVES MATTER! BLACK LIVES MATTER! FORWARD MARCH! FORWARD MARCH!" She nodded to Nina to start the video, and the screen flashed from the slideshow to Folami, her beauty captivating, her words clear and true and harrowing.

"Rekia Boyd. Shot in the back of the head by an off-duty police officer in Chicago," the video began.

Toya handed Folami her bullhorn and grabbed the handle of the wagon with her camera and flyers. Folami, Nina, and Ray began reading the names of those killed by police. They read the names in unison at first, the sound carrying and echoing with a metallic crispness. Then, as they began walking, their rhythm disjointed. The refrain of names became a haunting chorus, highs and lows, up-tempo and down-tempo, names echoed and bouncing off each other, creating a brilliant cacophony that demanded attention and was sure to rile spirits.

The procession was purposefully slow. Toya, Folami, and Nina calling out names and glancing back every now and again to make sure the people stayed with them. A few people with banners followed behind them, the wagon with the projector pulled by a young woman in combat boots and gold stretch pants, her T-shirt boasting the Mexican flag. She pulled the wagon slowly, and the three young men carrying the sheet-turned-screen followed a few feet behind her.

Ray had dropped back. He bounced around the rear of their parade, chanting the names and "Black Lives Matter!" in alternate bursts. Pumping his fist and hyping up the foot soldiers who hoisted signs and handed out flyers along the way as people came out of their homes to watch and join.

Toya looked back and saw a small group of people, Fishbone leading them across the street, leave the tent and truck to join the march. She smiled and pumped her fist in his direction.

Fishbone smiled back, pounded his heart with palm, then held his fist up high. "ALL BLACK LIVES MATTER! ALL BLACK LIVES MATTER!" He yelled it loud as he could while holding up his pants and jogging to catch up. Red, jogging too with her red braids bouncing behind her, yelled too. "ALL BLACK LIVES MATTER!"

Toya pulled the wagon, fighting the urge to take out her camera and take shots of the eclectic mix of people who held up signs and raised their voices behind her. She glanced over at Folami, who cried but tried to smile while reading the names from the sheet. She dropped the paper to her thighs, the names rolling off her tongue like she was possessed. Nina yelled the names into the bullhorn. The chanting and signs commanding attention, the videos and slideshows playing on repeat, the group had grown in number as they made their way to Williams Park. Cars honked in support, drivers and passengers yelling "Black Lives Matter!" and "GOD BLESS YOU!" from their windows.

When they crossed the street, some people honked angrily, laying on their horns and yelling curses from their cars. The marchers pressed on though, unfazed and determined.

Reaching Fourth Street marked a shift in the tone. What had been passionate and decidedly upbeat became tense and infinitely more risky.

Lining Williams Park on the north and south sides were rows of St. Petersburg police in full riot gear. They stood at attention, chests protruding with bulletproof padding, legs covered in knee-high boots, their thick plastic body shields creating a protective wall, their batons at the ready and the sunlight glinting off their black helmets. Toya turned to face the group, walking backward and pulling the wagon slowly. She tried to make eye contact with as many of them as possible, wanting to send them love and courage, and needing to show them that she was with them every step of the way.

"BLACK LIVES MATTER!"

"NO JUSTICE, NO PEACE!"

"RACISM IS FEAR AND HATE. NO ONE'S SAFE IN A POLICE STATE!

"BLACK LIVES MATTER!"

"NO JUSTICE, NO PEACE!"

The chants picked up fervor, voices rising in determination and fear. The lines blurred, but no one cared. They pressed on. They crossed Fourth Street, stopping traffic as they walked and chanted, fists and signs in the air. There were no buses surrounding the park as usual, meaning the police must have caught wind of their plans and prepared themselves for a clash. The protestors made their way into the park, the overflow blocking the surrounding streets. They spread out, and Toya realized how large the march had grown.

What began as a hundred people on a corner had expanded to over five hundred people. Folami looked across the park and the street. Her bullhorn slowly dropping as she too became aware of how many people had joined them during their march. People had gotten out of their cars, climbed off the bus, come out of their homes, walked off their jobs. There were people in suits and people in housecoats, children on bikes and teenagers on skateboards. People with name tags pinned on stained Polo shirts stood alongside people in sundresses and shorts sets. The sun shone across the multitude of them, and when their voices rose up in protest, the heavens shook.

"BLACK LIVES MATTER!"

"NO JUSTICE, NO PEACE!"

"RACISM IS FEAR AND HATE. NO ONE'S SAFE IN A POLICE STATE!

"BLACK LIVES MATTER!"

"NO JUSTICE, NO PEACE!"

As the people swarmed the park, spilling into the streets and stopping traffic, drivers grew impatient. Angry horn blasts and irritated tourists headed to Beach Drive for shopping and access to the pier amped up the crowd. A couple in matching straw fedoras and bright, beach blue shorts pushed past two young girls holding up a poster of Tamir Rice.

"Don't run over them babies like that!" someone shouted.

"Fuck you!" the man said, grabbing his wife's hand and picking up their pace on the sidewalk.

"GET THE FUCK OUT OF THE STREET!" a woman yelled from her Benz. She blasted her horn.

A man in a green kufi slapped his hand on her hood. She blasted her horn and revved her engine. He slapped her car again.

People opened their car doors, yelling curses at the protestors. "GET THE FUCK OUT OF THE STREET!" and "MOVE, ASSHOLE!" challenged the chants of "BLACK LIVES MATTER" and "NO JUSTICE, NO PEACE!" More passersby barreled through protestors who took up room on the sidewalk. At least three separate shoving matches ensued. A couple of police officers moved from their formation and went over to the minor scuffles. They grabbed at a protestor and pushed him down. He stood up and held his hands up in surrender. A woman with a sign that read "Stop Police Brutality" walked up to the officers still in line and screamed in their faces.

"STOP KILLING UNARMED CITIZENS! STOP KILLING UNARMED CHILDREN!" she screamed, shaking her sign in their faces. One of the officers pushed her with his shield and she fell down. A few protestors helped her up while two others pulled the lids off the small cans of paint they held and threw the red paint across four police officers in a row.

The red splashed across their shields and the face guards on their helmets. They stood stunned for a moment, then, in what looked like a rehearsed response, the entire row of officers jutted their shields forward, knocking all the protestors in front of them to the ground.

The other protestors reacted, screaming and pushing, grabbing at the cans of paint and prying off the lids as fast as they could.

Toya looked at Folami. "You ready?" she said.

Folami took a deep breath and nodded. She raised the bullhorn to her mouth and continued saying the names. Nina followed suit. Toya put her camera bag across her shoulder and grabbed flyers from the box. She recruited five protestors to take some flyers and they took to the street. They put flyers on windshields and stuffed them in the hands of people standing outside their cars or hanging out their windows. Even the people who were upset and cursing got a flyer jammed into their hands or slid into their car. A group of protestors had put their signs down and linked arms, blocking the traffic across Fourth Street and across Third Street. Cars snaked around the Williams Park. Workers and customers came running out of nearby restaurants and stores. Some of them took off their aprons and joined in, picking up discarded signs and blending in to the melee. Shoppers clutched their bags and stared in horror.

A few protestors had covered themselves in red paint. They mixed in with people on the street and those protesting, red paint transferring to passersby and other protestors like a contaminated crime scene. One of the men who had been carrying the screen grabbed two cans of paint and flung them into the air over a group of police who had forced a woman to the ground. The red paint flew out of the can and hovered for a moment before splashing down, the cans smacking against their helmets. The sound set off a chain reaction.

Uncapped cans of paint, red splashing over the rim, were hurled into the air by other protestors. The paint rained down on protestors, cars, drivers, passersby, and police alike. Paint, red as blood, slashed across signs and posters, the portraits becoming more symbolic than ever as the black-and-white photos were assaulted with angry red. Blood across faces on the posters, blood across the faces and bodies of the protestors, all too real, all too loud and accusatory. As the cans came crashing down, smashing windshields and cracking against helmets and police shields, the paint ignited the police the way blood ignites wolves.

Two officers who had been hit by cans of paint took off their helmets, covered in paint as they were, and struggled to their feet. Once righted, they drew their firearms. They pointed their guns at the nearest group of protestors. The teenagers at the end of their gun barrels held their signs in front of them and screamed. A group of other protestors, led by Fishbone and Red, ran in the direction of the screams. They held up their signs and surrounded the teenagers.

"You gon' shoot these kids! You gon' shoot these kids!" Fishbone yelled. "I know you ain't gon' shoot these kids!"

Red held a poster of Aiyana Jones and thrust it at one of the officers who pointed a gun in their direction. "You like killin' kids! You like killin' kids!" she screamed at the officer.

Folami called out to Toya, waving her over to help her with an older woman who had been knocked down by an officer. Toya shifted her camera bag on her shoulder and ran to Folami. They helped the woman up together and lead her to a nearby bench. Several more police officers had taken out their guns. Folami wiped tears from her eyes.

"What do we do now? They're taking out their guns," Folami said.

"I don't know," Toya said. She looked around the park. Complete pandemonium ensued. Police forced protestors down to the ground, Tasers out and clubs swinging, ballistic shields thrusting against signs. "We can't stop now. Let's try to gain control. Let's try to organize, to centralize everyone here in the park."

"We can try, but these police smell blood," Folami said.

Nina came up with her bullhorn. "What's the plan?" She panted and wiped at the sweat running down her temples.

"We're going to try to reel people in. If we can get them to move into the center of the park, maybe we can gain some control. Reorganize for the long haul."

More police vans arrived on the scene, weaving through traffic and screeching to abrupt stops and jumping the curbs to the sidewalk.

"BACK AWAY FROM THE POLICE!" Nina yelled into the bullhorn.

"Back away from the police! BACK AWAY FROM THE POLICE!" Folami screamed into her bullhorn.

"BACK AWAY FROM THE POLICE! BACK AWAY FROM THE POLICE!" Protestors started to chant. Some of them moving back and disengaging as much they could. They huddled in small groups, making their way into the center of the park.

Police started arresting people, knees in their backs and plastic zip ties locking their hands in painful-looking angles. They opened the van doors. They carried and crammed people into the paddy wagons. A few protestors picked up cans of paint and instead of throwing them or flinging the paint into the air, they poured red on themselves.

"BLOOD! BLOOD! BLOOD!" the group of women from RiseUP! chanted. They covered themselves in red paint, held up their signs and posters, walked into the street. "BLOOD! BLOOD! BLOOD!" they yelled.

More police officers took out their firearms, commanding the women to get down on the ground. Toya ran over to them, pleading with them to get down.

"Get down! Just get down!"

"BLOOD, BLOOD, BLOOD!" the women continued to yell, two of them dropping to their knees. The others didn't yield. They hoisted their signs and screamed back at the officers.

"GET DOWN ON THE FUCKING GROUND!" the officers said.

Toya whipped around to see another group of officers taking out their guns and screaming at protestors to get down.

"NO ONE IS ARMED!" Folami said into her bullhorn. "NO ONE IS ARMED!"

Nina joined in, alternately yelling for the protestors to back away from the police and screaming to the police that no one was armed.

Toya slid her camera bag to the front of her and unzipped it. As protestors were arrested and others gathered in the center of the park, the police moved in. Some of them had their guns out; others had their Tasers held at their waists, and still others their batons raised.

The women in front of Toya had all dropped to their bellies, but they still screamed, "BLOOD!" The police still had their weapons drawn. One officer, his helmet coated on one side in red paint, his vest splattered with it, his eyes unblinking, wide and frantic, stepped over to the petite woman with the dreads. She screamed in that bigger than her body, bigger than life voice, "BLOOD!" The officer grabbed her dreads and yanked her head up, lowering his gun to her temple.

Toya looked down at her camera bag, compelled to capture the moment. The officer stood wide-legged, a grip of dreads dangling from one hand and his gun, steady and poised at the woman's temple. Her mouth open in fear, calling out, her arms stretched out at her sides, her hands trembling. It was all happening so fast, people running through the park, the other women screaming and crying for the officer to let their friend go. Toya looked all around her, faces and voices a blur of sight and sound. Everything distorted by rage and frustration, fear and desperation. The only thing clear was the police officer with his gun at the woman's head. That was the shot. That was the image. The one that would show the terror, the force, the brutality. The woman, unarmed and afraid, flailing about on the ground, holding her arms out, reaching out for mercy. The officer yanking her hair up, the force of it showing in his bulging neck and shoulders. The gun. The gun pointed at her head.

Toya had to document it. She had to get proof.

She unzipped her camera bag, the motion of her arms catching the officer's attention. An almost imperceptible glance in her direction. Rage and anger. Frustration and fear.

Toya had to capture it. She reached into her bag.

The officer whipped around, twisting his body and the gun in Toya's direction, releasing the woman's hair, all in one swift motion.

Toya pulled out her camera.

The officer pulled the trigger.

About the Author

A Milwaukee, Wisconsin, native, Sheree L. Greer hosts Oral Fixation, the only LGBTQ Open Mic series in Tampa Bay, teaches writing and literature at St. Petersburg College, and started The Kitchen Table Literary Arts Center to showcase and support the work of ancestor, elder, and contemporary women writers of color. Learn more about Sheree and her work at www.shereelgreer.com.

Books Available from Bold Strokes Books

24/7 by Yolanda Wallace. When the trip of a lifetime becomes a pitched battle between life and death, will anyone survive? (978-1-62639-6-197)

A Return to Arms by Sheree Greer. When a police shooting makes national headlines, activists Folami and Toya struggle to balance their relationship and political allegiances, a struggle intensified after a fiery young artist enters their lives. (978-1-62639-6-814)

After the Fire by Emily Smith. Paramedic Connor Haus is convinced her time for love has come and gone, but when firefighter Logan Curtis comes into town, she learns it may not be too late after all. (978-1-62639-6-524)

Dian's Ghost by Justine Saracen. The road to genocide is paved with good intentions. (978-1-62639-5-947)

Fortunate Sum by M. Ullrich. Financial advisor Catherine Carter lives a calculated life, but after a collision with spunky Imogene Harris (her latest client) and unsolicited predictions, Catherine finds herself facing an unexpected variable: Love. (978-1-62639-5-305)

Soul to Keep by Rebekah Weatherspoon. What *won't* a vampire do for love... (978-1-62639-6-166)

When I Knew You by KE Payne. Eight letters, three friends, two lovers, one secret. Can the past ever be forgiven? (978-1-62639-5-626)

Wild Shores by Radclyffe. Can two women on opposite sides of an oil spill find a way to save both a wildlife sanctuary and their hearts? (978-1-62639-6-456)

Love on Tap by Karis Walsh. Beer and romance are brewing for Tace Lomond when archaeologist Berit Katsaros comes into her life. (987-1-162639-564-0)

Love on the Red Rocks by Lisa Moreau. An unexpected romance at a lesbian resort forces Malley to face her greatest fears where she must choose between playing it safe or taking a chance at true happiness. (987-1-162639-660-9)

Tracker and the Spy by D. Jackson Leigh. There are lessons for all when Captain Tanisha is assigned untried pyro Kyle and a lovesick dragon horse for a mission to track the leader of a dangerous cult. (987-1-162639-448-3)

Whirlwind Romance by Kris Bryant. Will chasing the girl break Tristan's heart or give her something she's never had before? (987-1-162639-581-7)

Whiskey Sunrise by Missouri Vaun. Culture and religion collide when Lovey Porter, daughter of a local Baptist minister, falls for the handsome thrill-seeking moonshine runner, Royal Duval. (987-1-162639-519-0)

Dyre: By Moon's Light by Rachel E. Bailey. A young werewolf, Des, guards the aging leader of all the Packs: the Dyre. Stable employment—nice work, if you can get it…at least until silver bullets start to fly. (978-1-62639-6-623)

Fragile Wings by Rebecca S. Buck. In Roaring Twenties London, can Evelyn Hopkins find love with Jos Singleton or will the scars of the Great War crush her dreams? (978-1-62639-5-466)

Live and Love Again by Jan Gayle. Jessica Whitney could be Sarah Jarret's second chance at love, but their differences and Sarah's grief continue to come between their budding relationship. (978-1-62639-5-176)

Starstruck by Lesley Davis. Actress Cassidy Hayes and writer Aiden Darrow find out the hard way not all life-threatening drama is confined to the TV screen or the pages of a manuscript. (978-1-62639-5-237)

Stealing Sunshine by Tina Michele. Under the Central Florida sun, two women struggle between fear and love as a dangerous plot of deception and revenge threatens to steal priceless art and lives. (978-1-62639-4-452)

The Fifth Gospel by Michelle Grubb. Hiding a Vatican secret is dangerous—sharing the secret suicidal—can Felicity survive a perilous book tour, and will her PR specialist, Anna, be there when it's all over? (978-1-62639-4-476)

Cold to the Touch by Cari Hunter. A drug addict's murder is the start of a dangerous investigation for Detective Sanne Jensen and Dr. Meg Fielding, as they try to stop a killer with no conscience. (978-1-62639-526-8)

Forsaken by Laydin Michaels. The hunt for a killer teaches one woman that she must overcome her fear in order to love, and another that success is meaningless without happiness. (978-1-62639-481-0)

Infiltration by Jackie D. When a CIA breach is imminent, a Marine instructor must stop the attack while protecting her heart from being disarmed by a recruit. (978-1-62639-521-3)

Midnight at the Orpheus by Alyssa Linn Palmer. Two women desperate to make their way in the world, a man hell-bent on revenge, and a cop risking his career: all in a day's work in Capone's Chicago. (978-1-62639-607-4)

Spirit of the Dance by Mardi Alexander. Major Sorla Reardon's return to her family farm to heal threatens Riley Johnson's safe life when small-town secrets are revealed, and love may not conquer all. (978-1-62639-583-1)

Sweet Hearts by Melissa Brayden, Rachel Spangler, and Karis Walsh. Do you ever wonder *Whatever happened to...*? Find out when you reconnect with your favorite characters from Melissa Brayden's *Heart Block*, Rachel Spangler's *LoveLife*, and Karis Walsh's *Worth the Risk*. (978-1-62639-475-9)

Totally Worth It by Maggie Cummings. Who knew there's an all-lesbian condo community in the NYC suburbs? Join twentysomething BFFs Meg and Lexi at Bay West as they navigate friendships, love, and everything in between. (978-1-62639-512-1)

Illicit Artifacts by Stevie Mikayne. Her foster mother's death cracked open a secret world Jil never wanted to see…and now she has to pick up the stolen pieces. (978-1-62639-472-8)

Pathfinder by Gun Brooke. Heading for their new homeworld, Exodus's chief engineer Adina Vantressa and nurse Briar Lindemay carry game-changing secrets that may well cause them to lose everything when disaster strikes. (978-1-62639-444-5)

Prescription for Love by Radclyffe. Dr. Flannery Rivers finds herself attracted to the new ER chief, city girl Abigail Remy, and the incendiary mix of city and country, fire and ice, tradition and change is combustible. (978-1-62639-570-1)

Ready or Not by Melissa Brayden. Uptight Mallory Spencer finds relinquishing control to bartender Hope Sanders too tall an order in fast-paced New York City. (978-1-62639-443-8)

Summer Passion by MJ Williamz. Women loving women is forbidden in 1946 Hollywood, yet Jean and Maggie strive to keep their love alive and away from prying eyes. (978-1-62639-540-4)

The Princess and the Prix by Nell Stark. "Ugly duckling" Princess Alix of Monaco was resigned to loneliness until she met racecar driver Thalia d'Angelis. (978-1-62639-474-2)

Winter's Harbor by Aurora Rey. Lia Brooks isn't looking for love in Provincetown, but when she discovers chocolate croissants and pastry chef Alex McKinnon, her winter retreat quickly starts heating up. (978-1-62639-498-8)

The Time Before Now by Missouri Vaun. Vivian flees a disastrous affair, embarking on an epic, transformative journey to escape her past, until destiny introduces her to Ida, who helps her rediscover trust, love, and hope. (978-1-62639-446-9)

Twisted Whispers by Sheri Lewis Wohl. Betrayal, lies, and secrets—whispers of a friend lost to darkness. Can a reluctant psychic set things right or will an evil soul destroy those she loves? (978-1-62639-439-1)

The Courage to Try by C.A. Popovich. Finding love is worth getting past the fear of trying. (978-1-62639-528-2)

Break Point by Yolanda Wallace. In a world readying for war, can love find a way? (978-1-62639-568-8)

Countdown by Julie Cannon. Can two strong-willed, powerful women overcome their differences to save the lives of seven others and begin a life they never imagined together? (978-1-62639-471-1)

Keep Hold by Michelle Grubb. Claire knew some things should be left alone and some rules should never be broken, but the most forbidden, well, they are the most tempting. (978-1-62639-502-2)

Deadly Medicine by Jaime Maddox. Dr. Ward Thrasher's life is in turmoil. Her partner Jess left her, and her job puts her in the path of a murderous physician who has Jess in his sights. (978-1-62639-424-7)

New Beginnings by KC Richardson. Can the connection and attraction between Jordan Roberts and Kirsten Murphy be enough for Jordan to trust Kirsten with her heart? (978-1-62639-450-6)